Robyn

www.MarlonGreen.net

Other Books By Marlon Green
Making Love in the Rain
Twilight Moods (co-editor/author)

Coming Soon from
Greenday Publishing
Chloe Barksdale
and
Mind Evolution

MARLON GREEN

Butter

**IF YOU CAN'T BE WITH THE ONE YOU LOVE...
PREPARE FOR DRAMA!**

LOVELINE PAPERBACK FICTION

GREENDAY PUBLISHING

PG COUNTY, MD

LOVELINE PAPERBACK FICTION
GREENDAY PUBLISHING, INC
PO BOX 5362
LAUREL, MD 20726

First Loveline Paperback Fiction Edition 2004
Loveline Books is a division of Greenday Publishing, Inc.

Hardcover Art by Stephen Howard

Library of Congress Cataloging – in – Publication Data is available.

ISBN 0-9679377-6-0 (Pbk)

DEDICATION

To that man busy chasing sex

To that woman in love with the wrong man

To the person that takes his/her lover for granted

ACKNOWLEDGEMENTS

Heavenly Father, You make all of this possible. Though bruised, battered, and many times at the end of my rope with this hard hustle and struggle, my faith remains pure and true. To my mother, LeJuane Robinson, thank you and your husband, Jesse, for looking out for me and putting up with the habits, both good and bad, of an artist. You've always been in my corner, even when you thought I was crazier than I am. To my father, Luke Green, thanks for your wisdom and for looking out for me with your postal peeps. And my grandmother, Nancy Powell (Gramma, Junebug, Gee-Gee), thank you for always being there. I love you.

To all of the radio personalities that lent me a hand in reaching so many readers, I really appreciate the love and support. Barbara Reynolds, I owe my first radio appearance to you. Carlisle Sealy, Kimberly Washington, Joe Gorham, and Audrey Chapman at WHUR 96.3 FM, you all are a blessing. My XM peeps, Autumn Turner and Traci Jones, you have really treated me with remarkable kindness. I reciprocate the love. Michele Wright at WPGC 95.5 FM, thanks for welcoming me into the studio.

Jeannie Jones at 93.9 KISS, don't hold back, give me some love. Pamela, I need some from you, too.

Down in Charlotte, North Carolina, I have to give thanks to the Breakfast Brothers on Power 98 FM. Tone X, I still need some voice lessons. Janine Davis, I love those big brown eyes. You are so fine. No Limit Larry, keep holding it down.

Much love to DJ Curt on WTCC in Springfield, Massachusetts, and Jettie down in Tampa, Florida on WTMP. My girl Hodan with V-103, I'm waiting, sweetie. The Big Phat Morning Show up in Baltimore on 92 Q; Marc Clarke, Troy, and the lovely Marva, I'm on my way to see you.

I have to show some love for all of the stores that go above and beyond to make sure that readers, as well as authors, are taken care of; Brother Yao, Simba, and Lee McDonald at Karibu; Mr. Cliff at Expressions in Baltimore; Howard University Bookstore; Brother James at Dynasty Books; Reprint Books; Bruce at The Know; Marcus at Nubian Books; Tyrelle at Life Is A Box Of Crayons; Amir at The Shrine of the Black Madonna; N'Senga at African Spectrum; Felicia at Books For Thought; Emlyn at Mejah Books; and Ms. Margaret and Vell hustling in DC.

All of my girls with Our Conversation Piece Book Club (Cheryl and the rest of the wild bunch), y'all are off the hook. To all my girls down in Tampa in the R.E.A.P. Book Club (Kim, Alethea, Jennifer, Shana, and the crew), y'all know I'm coming back to see you, right? And my Circle of Sisters up in Kalamazoo (Sheletha, DaNikka, Tisha, Kizzy, Sue, Bonnie, and Connie), I'll be back for more shots and Spades.

Most of my love is for the thousands of women and men that have supported me and my literature. I'm here to make us happy. Keep enjoying me.

THANK YOU...

The kids in DC that had me as a teacher. I love you all.
Steve Howard for looking out for a brother.
George Gallop and Morris Gallop for having my back.
Keith, I love the cover. I'll have another for you soon.
Takisha for being such a true friend. I got your back.
Kimberly "Kimlove" Morsell for getting the word out.
Chris and Yolanda Clark for your constant love and support.
Bridgette Washington for taking good care of me in Atlanta.
Kato for being down with the struggle.
Leslie, thank you so much for being so special.
Crystal Wright for holding me down in Philly.
Rob Howard for telling the ladies and gents what to read.
Jami Williams and Tracy "Mind Evolution" Caldwell for
welcoming me in Hartford.
Butter for all of the memories and your friendship.
Mike, Danny, Hook, and the entire MD Ski-Express family.
Paul Gardner and the YLCP nation. We have to do business.
Samuel Bailey and MsDec25.
Lorraine Graham-Brown and WTTK.
Cocktails and the Live Poets down in Hotlanta.
James Lewis, holding down Reflections and New England.
Cha Ross-Estes, CEO of Why? Entertainment.
Shunda Blocker, Editor-in-Chief of Booking Matters.

Heavenly Father,

Another literary prayer is owed to You because You've brought me a long way since "The Rain." The blessings I've received are countless and the rewards are priceless. All of the glory is given to You. Saying that the past three years have been rough would be an understatement. My struggles have been bombs of reality. Nevertheless, my faith in You remains undeterred.

The least of my concerns are those that have hated or attempted to judge me; some not realizing that they weren't You. I pray that You bless them.

I thank You for allowing me to help so many people. I thank You for my gift of understanding and the ability to listen intently. It's hard being Marlon Green, but it's so much fun. Life is grand and I'm still "living."

Many would have mentally collapsed if they faced some of the hardships that I have. However, You've created a spiritual giant within me, which makes those hardships so small now that I look back. I even thank You for them because my wisdom has increased with each. Yes, life is grand and I owe it all to You.

Thank you, Lord.

Author's Note

I've been taken all around the world and I love it. A few women have taken me on cruises to the Caribbean, flights to Europe, and road trips to other states. Some have taken me to work with them and introduced me to their coworkers; I enjoyed meeting them. Then there are those that want me to accompany them to bed; sometimes we're alone, other times it's "Just Us Three." I've sat on nightstands, been held firmly on trains and buses, and snuggly placed into handbags. It is an honor to have my first book take "me" so many places.

I've had brothers tell me how I've helped them become more understanding, better communicators, and sensitive to the needs of a woman. Sisters have smiled and explained to me how I've brought new heights of sensuality to their minds, released traditional ties that bind, and provided them healthier paradigms. I'll bet that no author appreciates the love and support of his/her readers and reciprocates it as much as I do. I am actually a fan of my readers. They mean the world to me. The accolades are sweet and the handshakes and hugs only make things sweeter. God has blessed me with all of you so I now present the gift of Butter.

Butter

IF YOU CAN'T BE WITH THE ONE YOU LOVE...
PREPARE FOR DRAMA!

CHAPTER 1

Daren sat patiently waiting for Tamela, whom he called Butter, to page him. He gave her that nickname back when they used to date. Just like butter goes with everything from popcorn and vegetables, to oatmeal and grits, his *Butter* went well with everything that he wanted to do. If he asked her to play Scrabble, to watch the basketball game, to take a trip with him, go to a show, exercise together, or whatever his heart felt, she never harassed him; she would simply participate and go with the flow and enjoy every minute of it. She never was the type to bring the drama or the nagging with her. This also applied to everything that his freaky side wanted. Butter always rose to the occasion and handled her business.

Not even a Friday night with the fellas watching the game could take his mind off of Butter's wedding, which was less than 24 hours away. He knew that her wedding was inevitable, but being a die-hard romantic forced him to believe that his soul mate would call him at the last minute and tell him that she cancelled the wedding to be with him.

As his thoughts continued on the wedding, Daren began to replay the scenes from the day he and Tamela parted, the day she didn't act like Butter, the day that altered their lives. As he relived the day of the picnic that drew them apart, the vivid memory was interrupted by the cheers of amazement at Shaquille O'Neal's dunk.

"Damn! Did you see that? None of them bammas can mess with Shaq!" yelled Ted as he jumped out of his seat. "And I wanted Jalen Rose to get a ring, too."

Daren smiled as the dunk was replayed in slow motion. He was busy reminiscing the times he and Butter would play nude Nerf basketball in her bedroom. While watching the Chicago Bulls, between their love making session, Daren jumped from the bed, grabbed the Nerf basketball, and tried his best to imitate the shot that Michael Jordan made. As he shot the ball toward the Nerf basketball court on the back of the door, the ball was suddenly coming in his direction. Butter had jumped from the bed and blocked his shot. Within seconds they both wrestled and play fought as they tried to beat one another in Nerf basketball without any clothes on. The winner got the choice of what position they would do first once the love making started again. They always had a ball.

"That's Butter! That's my baby," Daren said as he grabbed his pager. At that moment he thought about settling down and marrying her.

Ted looked at Daren with disturbed eyes. "Man, why you wanna be bothered with her? That was way back in 1996."

Daren gave a slight frown and awaited an answer on the other end of the line.

"Hello?"

"What's up?" Daren asked as he hid the surprise in his voice. He easily recognized the voice of Butter's closest friend Robin. All he needed to hear was that the wedding was cancelled.

"You know Tamela is getting married tomorrow, right?"

"Yes," Daren answered as he walked away from the fellas to hear every word Robin was saying.

"Well, she's having a party tonight and she wants you to come."

"Is she still getting married?"

"Didn't I just say she's getting married tomorrow? Are you deaf or just in denial?"

"Whatever. Anyway, where's the party and who's there?"

"Just our closest friends and some entertainment."

"Strippers?"

"Look, are you coming or not? Just say that you're not, please."

Daren sensed there was something bothering Robin. He had known her since the 3rd grade and they had been friends ever since. She normally was jovial and very inviting, always cracking jokes with Daren and enjoying herself. "I'll be there. But tell me this, why do you have an attitude?"

"I have an attitude?"

"Yes, you do. You keep getting smart and everything. Do you care to tell me why?"

"I apologize. You know how I feel about the institution of marriage, don't you?"

"Yes," Daren said as he anxiously awaited her next statement.

"Well, if Tamela or Butter, whatever you call her, is so in love with her fiancé, then she wouldn't have made me promise to call you. She shouldn't be thinking about you or trying to see you either."

"She thinks about me that much?" Daren asked trying to get more information on Butter.

"Yes, and you better not say anything either."

"I'm not going to say anything. What does she say about me?"

"She keeps saying that she wishes she was marrying you. I keep telling her that if she isn't feeling her husband like that then she should call off the wedding."

Daren peeked around the corner to glance at the game. "Why does she want me at the party?"

"Look, Daren, don't play dumb with me. She wants to have sex with you one last time."

"Oh, really?"

"Yes, really. Why don't you just marry her, Daren? If you would just propose then she won't make this mistake."

"Won't make what mistake?"

"I think her getting married is a mistake. But I don't want any drama so I'm done trying to change her mind. However, I'm not done with you. Just say you aren't coming because I don't think it would be right if you did. I don't want anything bad to come on you or me, and more importantly - I don't want any drama," Robin said with a stern tone.

"You know damn well that I have too much class to do something like that."

"Daren, Tamela has class, too. But she's just hooked on you. I don't know what you did to her, but -"

"Oh, you know what I did to her," Daren chuckled with sarcasm.

"Yeah, yeah, I know; the balcony in Ocean City, the paints, the truck, and making love in the rain."

"Yes, making love in the rain. We had a good -"

"Daren!"

"Oh, I got a little carried away."

"You aren't coming, right?"

"No, I'm coming now."

"Daren, don't do this."

"I'm not going to mess with her. I just have to pick up something in your area. Haven't you known me over 20 years?"

"Yeah, yeah, whatever. We were in Mrs. Jenkins' 3rd grade class together. Look, I don't have time to go into all of that right now."

"And remember we kissed?"

Robin became embarrassed. The memory of that kiss was always in the back of her head, but she nor Daren ever brought it up in conversation since he and Butter got together. Deep down inside, Robin wanted to make love to Daren. She held a place in her heart for him since their kiss in elementary school and all through high school. Now, 10 years later, she still wanted him, but she would not dare touch him out of respect for her best friend. She decided long ago to never tell a soul - not even Daren had a clue as to her secret longing.

"Is everybody there, now?" Daren asked.

"Everybody but Butter."

"Is she on her way?"

"She said she'll be here around 10:00-10:30."

"I'm on my way."

"I mean what I said. Don't try to get with her, Daren. You shouldn't come at all."

"I'll make my pick-up and be gone. It'll only take 5 minutes."

"What do you want to pick up, a plate of food?"

"You know it, baby. Fix me two of 'em."

Daren didn't waste any time jumping on his motorcycle and driving the three-mile distance to Robin's house. He had one thing on his mind and only one woman knew his intentions, however, she didn't know that he would act so soon. Daren slowly drove down Robin's street looking for Butter's car. Not finding it, he strolled into Robin's back door, which accessed the kitchen.

"Boy, you scared me!" yelled a lovely almond toned woman. Her body was fit and her appearance caused many heads to turn in her direction - both men and women. Her name is Ebony.

"Shhh! Quiet down," said Daren. "Where's your sister?"

"Who? Robin?"

Daren paused and gave her a frown with a slight smile. It was known to make people feel stupid for their words or actions. In this case it was done because Ebony only had one sister. She smiled once she caught his smirk.

"She's in there. Want me to get her?"

"No. Where did she put my two plates?" Daren asked as he looked around the kitchen and then to his watch. Time was of the essence and he knew he had to move quickly.

"Your plates are in that bag right beside you."

"Okay, let's go."

Ebony looked at Daren like he was crazy.

"Let's go where? I can't leave. You have lost your mind."

"Is that right?"

"Yeah, that's right."

"Look, Robin has everything done. What are you doing?"

"I'm helping with the food."

"All of the food looks done to me," Daren said holding up his bag.

"I have to serve it," Ebony said trying to dispel his statement.

"This isn't a children's party. They can fix their own plates."

"I have to make the drinks, too," Ebony shot back.

Daren looked past Ebony and focused on the contents on the counter and then to the huge wooden spoon in her hand. "Kool-Aid? You're in here making red Kool-Aid?"

As Ebony began to laugh with one hand on the counter while bending over, Daren slowed down his words and got serious.

"Ebony, this is our chance to do what we've been looking forward to. I'm walking out of this door and it would mean a lot to us both if you were to leave with me. I even brought the spare helmet."

Ebony's eyes lit up. "You brought the motorcycle?"

"Of course. Now let's go riding before your sister comes in here."

"Daren, you know I want to, but I can't. That's my sister's friend."

"Is she your friend?"

"Hell no! I just don't want to put Robin in an awkward position."

"You won't because she won't know. We'll have a ball. Let's go."

"I'm sure we would've had a ball. The time is just not right. Where were you going to take me anyway?"

"I was going to take you to...remember that night we were playing *truth or dare* and you talked about your biggest fantasy?"

"Yes. The one about doing it on a -"

"Yes, that one. I was taking you to meet that fantasy."

"Tonight? You are going to do that to-night?"

Daren gave her a look of sincerity and held the door open.

Ebony placed the wooden spoon on the counter, grabbed her pocketbook, and walked out of the back door with Daren. "They can make their own damn Kool-Aid," she said and Daren closed the door.

As they sat in their seats and buckled their belts, Daren began reading a magazine while Ebony gazed at him from her window seat. Forty-five minutes into the flight he observed the lonely stewardess resting in the front of the plane. He also observed the passengers' heads, which were nestled against a pillow, a headrest, or a window as they slept with the lights off. Daren could not help but to feel like a genius for getting seats in the last row. There wasn't anyone sitting across the aisle, either.

Daren quietly removed his seat belt and sat on the floor in front of his seat. He then leaned his head over and began licking the inside of Ebony's knees. Her body jolted from surprise for a second as she awakened. Noticing her fantasy taking place before her eyes, she closed her knees, eased up, pulled her panties down, and allowed Daren to pull them completely off and he stuffed them into his pocket. She then parted her legs and relaxed her head as she ignored the threat of someone watching. When she fantasized, she never imagined the visions in her mind to ever become reality. Now, thousands of feet in the skies above West Virginia, she was realizing the beginning of a fantasy and she felt that her fears wouldn't stop it.

"Mmm, Daren," Ebony heard herself whisper as Daren's tongue met the lips of her vagina. He outlined them slowly as if he and Ebony were alone and had absolutely all of the time that they needed. As she felt his tongue enter her vagina, she tried to envision where his tongue was traveling and how it looked from his view. Suddenly she felt the tip of his tongue wiggle against the left wall of her vagina.

"That's mama's sugar walls," Ebony said as she relaxed again. She never had her walls licked so she concentrated on the feeling. She became so relaxed that she could feel moisture running down to her ass. Seconds later she felt Daren's tongue ease to the destination of the wetness and redirect it to his throat using his tongue as a transport. With a deep swallow he patted his tongue rapidly against his lips.

"Ebony, you taste like roses," Daren whispered as he did a once over with his tongue to make sure no wetness existed beyond her lips. He then swallowed her natural juices slowly and seductively.

"You are so nasty," Ebony chuckled while she imagined how roses tasted. As Daren held her legs by the back of her knees she relaxed them. After several minutes of licking Ebony's walls, Daren suddenly shifted to her clitoris. Jolts of sensuous spasms raced around her midsection. This new feeling prompted Ebony to open her eyes once again to visually grasp her fantasy. Her eyes were greeted with the light blue moonlight shining off Daren's chocolate, bald head.

"This is real," Ebony whispered to herself as she closed her eyes.

Daren began imagining that he was French kissing Vivica Fox while his tongue slowly and seductively stroked Ebony's clit. As Daren's kisses evolved into soft tongue slaps against the sides of Ebony's clit, she began to gyrate. As the soft chants of an orgasm grew to screams of a climax, Ebony grabbed Daren's head with both hands and looked out of the window. Her eyes wearily focused on the beautiful site of the moon, the moonlit skies, and the clouds as she came.

Daren eased into his seat with stiffness in his left side and his jaw. The hips that he had just made dance scooted past him and went into the restroom. Seconds later Ebony whispered into his right ear. "I appreciate the tongue lashing you gave me, but that was only half of my fantasy," she said pulling Daren into the restroom. Once inside, Daren motioned for Ebony to bend over. "I am not touching that toilet," Ebony said.

Daren smiled and Ebony smiled with him. He then turned her around and lifted her right leg to her side and placed it on the middle of the door. She then placed her left hand on the wall opposite the door and her right hand on the wall between them above the sink. Daren quickly slipped on a condom and began hitting it from the back.

The two walked out of the heated box as if everything was normal. The woman waiting to use the restroom rushed into it. Minutes later she appeared with embarrassment on her face and said, "Excuse me. May I use that rose scented spray that you used in the restroom, please?"

"No," Daren answered. "We used it all."

As the woman walked away the funk hit their noses. "Damn!" Daren exclaimed. "What did she eat for lunch today? Chittlin' soup?" Ebony couldn't hold back her laugh as Daren frowned. Daren smiled because he believed that he was finally over Butter.

CHAPTER 2

Butter, with her beautiful face, 5'4" frame, and thick body, sat on her mother's bed with a look of concern on her light face. Her wedding day was going as planned. The groom and groomsmen had arrived at the hotel dressed and ready to go, while the bridal party had transformed her mother's living room into a dressing room. They all attended the bridal shower the night before and migrated in the wee hours of the morning to rest in their temporary dressing room. Nevertheless, Butter was very concerned and only Robin was there to console her.

"Girl, what is wrong with you?"

"You know what's wrong," Butter said calmly as she looked at Robin through her glasses. "I'm getting married to one man, but my heart belongs to another man. You know exactly what's wrong."

"Don't you think you let this wedding thing get a little too far feeling the way you're feeling? I mean, for real, you never stopped loving Daren. Why would you let this thing with Donald get to this point?"

"Because I can't continue to wait on Daren. I have a child that needs the presence of a strong man in the home. I also want a house and another child. And as a woman I have needs."

"So," Robin said frowning.

"So Donald has stepped up to the plate and he is meeting my needs."

"But do you love him?"

"Yes, I do."

"Are you in love with him?"

"Yes."

"More than Daren?" Robin asked with a sneaky expression across her creamy-brown face.

Butter looked at her like she was insane. "Are you crazy? There ain't but one Daren. Donald doesn't come close to being as much fun as Daren. Daren will have you laughing all the time, and he's always getting me to do something that's new and adventurous. Plus, he is a conversationalist when it's time to be serious. He knows my heart. He ain't afraid to -"

"...will join hands in that old Negroid spiritual, free at last, free at last. Thank God almighty, we are free at last. Never mind the speech." Both women begin to laugh and

Robin begins to speak seriously. "Tamela, do you hear yourself? You never brag about your fiancé, but you speak about your ex-lover like he's a god."

Butter looked at herself in the mirror. Her smile, from speaking about Daren, transformed into a look of concern. Within seconds she was reliving the night she and Daren saw their painted bodies in the mirror of her darkened room. A smile immediately came to her face. "Robin, remember the time when Daren painted my body and -"

"You are seriously in denial."

"Why didn't he come see me last night? Robin, it's been so long since I've seen him. If I could have seen him, then I would have been able to tell if he wants me." Butter was staring off into space as she spoke.

Robin felt sorry for her friend. After thinking about her sister Ebony's return from her fantasy flight, she felt even sorrier. It was clear to her that Daren was giving up on Butter. She knew that Butter had given up on Daren long ago. However, Daren was embedded in her soul permanently, and it would take a hell of a man to make her forget him completely. "Tamela, he did come over, but you weren't there yet."

"Did you see him? You called him for me, didn't you?"

Robin became nervous with the thought of calling Daren for Butter, but not wanting him to come to her party. "Yes, I called him and he came over," Robin said looking away from Butter.

Butter sat up and gave Robin her complete attention. "What did he have on? What did he say? Was he looking fine as usual? Tell me, girl!"

Robin tried to choose her words carefully. "Well, he asked me to fix him a couple of plates so I told Ebony to do it for me. When I came back into the kitchen they were gone."

"What? The plates?"

"Yes, the plates, my sister, and Daren," Robin said while looking down at her own dress.

Butter began to analyze the previous night's attendees. "She didn't even tell you she was leaving? She always did want Daren anyway."

"He has moved on, Tamela, just like you said you were doing years ago. You have a lifetime of memories. Now sit back and think about why you're wearing that wedding dress. Think about that handsome man at the hotel waiting for you to walk down the aisle." Robin was growing more disgusted with Butter's behavior and she was tired of talking about Daren altogether.

Butter thought about Robin's statements long and hard. As much as it hurt her, the truth was that she was getting married and about to start a new life with a new man.

"Tamela, why did y'all break up in the first place?"

"It was stupid. It really was. Stupid and petty. We never were really together, but it was almost as if we were. After we came back from Ocean City I took him to a picnic. He knew a lot of the people there, which included some women. He went over there and played cards and stuff and left me."

"Is that it? Did he ask you to come over and play cards?"

"Yes, but I didn't want to."

"So that's it?"

"Not really."

"Well, hurry up, Tammy, and tell the story."

"I went crazy on him when we left. I don't know what was wrong with me. I just loved him so much, but my words came out the wrong way. I kind of disrespected him and we stopped kickin' it from that point on. We'd talk some every now and then, but we no longer went out and we didn't have sex anymore."

The house phone began ringing and Robin answered.

"Tamela, your son is at the hotel with your fiancé, but he is not listening to him."

"Tell them that we're on our way."

The two women grabbed their things and headed out the room to round up the other ladies so that they could all go to the hotel. Once in the Cadillac, being chauffeured

by Robin, Butter asked for her cellular phone.
Robin handed it to her not knowing what was
coming next.

"Daren, I hope that you had a good
time last night. You should have come to my
party and stayed. We had a lot of fun, but I
guess that this is it. You're free to do what
you want and so am I. Enjoy your life."

As Butter hung up the phone, Robin
started to get on her about making such a
pointless call, but she couldn't help but to
feel sorry for the sniffles that she heard. The
low-toned sobs from her best friend hurt her
to her heart. Robin wanted to turn the car
around so they could get some money from a
money machine and drive to Atlantic City for
a week. She would do anything to avoid her
friend making a huge mistake like marrying
the wrong man. Instead, Robin simply turned
the volume to the radio up a few notches.

Walking into the hotel's main entrance
they found Butter's son sitting with her
fiancé's sister. Butter couldn't help but to be
overly concerned after seeing her son's tears
and his pouting lips. "Billy, why are you crying? I have him, Melissa," Butter said as she
gave a faint smile to her soon to be sister-
in-law. She then looked back at her son. "Billy,
what's going on?"

"Donald wouldn't let me in the room
with his friends. We...we...we were in there
and then he put me out. He wouldn't let me
watch Pokémon or Dragonball-Z, either!"

"Why did he put you out? Were you acting up?"

"No, I...I was sitting there and one of them started smoking a cigarette and Donald said I had to leave. He said for me to go to Ms. Melissa's room because of the smoke. I told him that I smelled smoke before and he said this was the new smoke."

Butter became enraged. She just knew that her soon to be husband wasn't smoking marijuana around her son. She felt that he shouldn't be smoking at all. As she looked at the *Your husband ain't shit* expression on Robin's face, she became angrier. "Melissa, where's his room?"

"You can't see the groom before the wedding. Your son is okay now."

"I'll show you where his room is, Mommy," Billy said trying to lead her there.

Melissa looked at Billy then back to Butter. "Tamela, you can't go up there. I'll tell you what, call him on his cell phone 'cause you know it's bad luck for the bride to see the groom on their wedding day."

Butter looked around as Melissa's words sunk in. She wasn't at all a violent woman. In fact, she was the sweetest woman most had ever met. However, when it came to her son she would hurt somebody. "Robin, take Billy and wash his face, please." She then whipped out her cell phone. "And, Billy, take off those Nikes and put on your dress shoes."

"I don't need them 'cause I ain't carry-

ing no stupid ring for you to get married."
Billy ran down the hall as fast as he could.

"I got him, girl. Don't worry," Robin said
as she kicked off her heels and grabbed the
sides of her dress. She then took off running
after Billy. She never thought that being the
bridesmaid would include these wild episodes.
First she had to deal with her sister Ebony
going out with Daren, then Butter talking
about Daren all morning, now chasing and
cleaning up Billy.

Butter pressed send and waited for her
fiancé's voice.

"Hello?"

"Donald!"

"Naw, dis ain't Donald. Who dis?"

"This is his got damn fiancée – the one
that paid for that gift that you and your friends
received."

"Oh, Tammy! My bad. Thanks for the
cologne. Dat shit is expensive! Hold on."

Butter became even angrier after hearing Troy's voice. *Of all of Donald's friends,
why did Troy have to answer the phone?* she
thought.

"Yeah, what's up, baby?"

"Don't baby me, got-damnit! You're up
there smokin' weed before we get married?
On our wedding day? And why in the hell did
you put my son out?"

"I am not smoking and I didn't put your
son out. I told him to go to Melissa's room."

"Why?"

"Because Mike wanted to smoke some weed. I didn't smoke any chronic, it was just Mike and 'em."

"You chose your friends over my son?"

"No, I didn't. I didn't want him around the smoke so I told him to go to Melissa's. Don't even try to make a big deal out of this."

"You need to start checking your boys and start acting responsibly."

"What are you talking about? Ain't nobody even do nothin' wrong!" Donald said raising his voice.

"Donald, if Mike wanted to smoke you should have told him to do it outside of the room. That's number one. Number two, you are supposed to be bonding with my son and setting a better example of a man because in less than an hour he will be *our* son. Number three, your bachelor party is over and so is your life as a single man. You can't sit around with your immature friends and smoke. Your life is changing now. Number four -"

"Number four? You mean -"

"Wait a minute, let me finish! Number four, you and the groomsmen are not going to be smelling like weed at my wedding. I suggest you put that shit out, open those windows, and leave so that you won't be funky. You also owe my son an apology. He is upset because -" Butter heard the phone go dead. "Hello? Donald!"

As far as Donald was concerned the conversation was over. However, his hanging up the phone gave Butter more to think about. It was almost a half an hour before the ceremony was to start and she still had to talk with her son, make sure the bridesmaids were straight, and then make sure that her own things were together. She looked at Melissa, whom she really didn't have a strong relationship with, and headed toward the bridesmaids' dressing room.

It was almost 3:00 and time for the wedding to begin. Butter and her bridesmaids lined up in sequence awaiting the music from the keyboardist. She then saw the only missing member to her party come down the hallway without her son, Billy. Robin whispered to Butter that she couldn't clean Billy's face because he ran into the men's room and wouldn't come out.

For a few minutes Butter remained silent. She considered getting her little brother to carry the ring, but decided against it because he was 12-years-old. She felt that he was too big to be cute like her 6-year-old son. She then thought about having Robin carry the ring and slip it to the best man, however, her thoughts led her back to her son and his well-being. When the wedding planner told her five minutes before ceremony, Butter ran down the hall to get Billy.

Once Butter got to the men's room door she paused to calm herself, to gather her thoughts, and to think of the right words to say to make Billy feel better and to convince him to participate. Slowly pushing the door open, she felt a shortness of breath at the sight before her. Kneeling down in front of her son was Daren. He had washed Billy's face and was now cheering him on and encouraging him to participate in the wedding.

"You got that, don't you?" Daren asked.

"Yes, Loco," Billy responded.

"Alright," Daren replied, "now get in there and make your mother happy. She deserves the best. And don't give your stepfather any problems, either. If he smokes a cigarette with the new smoke just leave the room because it's bad for your little brain."

"Okay. Hey, Loco! You played football with me, but you never played baseball with me."

"Tell me my favorite football team and I'll play baseball with you one day," Daren said.

"The Oakland Raiders. I like them, too."

Daren smiled and rubbed Billy's head. He then went into his pocket and pulled out a dollar. "Now, Billy, don't get any chocolate candy from that machine because it will mess up your white suit. Get some of those Starbursts or Skittles or something like that. You understand?"

"Yes," Billy yelled and he took the dollar. "Are you going to take me to a baseball game because stupid Donald won't take me?" Daren gave Billy a stern look and Billy withered. "I won't call him stupid anymore, Loco."

"You better not. Now get out of here. I'll see about taking you to a baseball game one day, but only if you're good."

"I'm going to be good. Bye, Loco," Billy said as he raced out the door. Upon seeing his mother he stopped in his tracks and lowered his head. "I apologize for not making you happy, Mommy. I'll be nice to Donald if it will make you happy."

Butter felt tears coming to her eyes, but she didn't really know why. She didn't know if it was his apology or his not being nice to Donald in the past that warranted the tears. She then considered that they may have been because of how she just heard how Daren and Billy talked and respected one another. She couldn't deny how easily Daren got through to Billy. "Mommy accepts your apology. Now go on and get your candy."

Billy ran back the opposite way and opened the bathroom door. "Hey, Loco, wash my mommy's face, too, please!" and he ran and bought his Skittles.

"Take a few now and save the rest for after the wedding," Butter ordered.

"Okay," Billy replied and before he could get four steps away from her, he poured half of the pack into his mouth and began chewing. Butter snatched the pack from him and Billy ran down the hall. As she watched him run toward Robin, her mind was jolted back to reality by the opening of the restroom door.

"Well, hello there. And may I say I've never seen a more beautiful bride."

Butter's head turned in the direction of the too familiar voice – the one voice that moved her like no other. However, her body froze. "What are you doing here?" she asked while handing him the Skittles. She loved the way he looked in his suit and tie.

"I'm here to look reality in the eye and to let it sink in. Are you okay?"

"Yes, Daren."

"You can't be. The groom is handsome and all, but where's the limousine?"

"We don't need a limo, Daren."

"This is not the wedding that you wanted. You always talked about getting married in a church, not a hotel. His uncle is driving y'all from the hotel in his Cadillac?"

Butter would have had some curse words for anyone else, but Daren's sarcasm always made her laugh. "Who told you that?" she asked with a big grin on her face.

"You know who told me. Billy did. Anyway, I hope that he takes good care of you. Here," Daren said while extending a pack of Starburst to her.

"You are so silly," Butter said as she put two into her mouth. "You ain't forget about me and my Starburst, huh?"

"You know I couldn't do that." Daren smiled and prepared himself to leave.

"Wait. What did you mean when you said 'look reality in the eye and let it sink in'?" Butter asked.

"Just making sure it's over. And, although I'm not a part of your wedding, I

wouldn't miss your special day for the world."
They both looked at each other for a few
seconds, then Daren pulled Butter into his
arms as he sensed her tears once again form-
ing. "It's okay, Butter. Butter, it's okay."

"Stop calling me that. Please don't call
me that."

"Okay, baby, but be patient with your
son. Just work with him and make sure he's
attended to."

"Yes, Daren," Butter said as she grew
more comfortable with her head against his
chest. As his arms securely squeezed, she
was suddenly reminded of what once was as
well as being reminded of everything she
missed in her love life.

"Baby, pull yourself together and walk
down the aisle."

"I am, Daren. Just hold me. Keep holding me."

Daren loved Butter's scent. It reminded
him of late nights in her bed because her
sheets gave off the same perfume. He wanted
to pour out his heart and tell her to leave out
the back door with him. There was so much
he wanted to express, but he didn't want to
destroy her wedding day and upset her friends
and family. As Butter continued to cry, Daren
grabbed some tissue and told her to blow
into it. She did so like a child.

"Thank you for talking to my son."

"No problem, cutie. Now go before they
come looking for you."

Butter gave Daren a long hug and got on her tippy-toes to kiss him on his cheek. As she left they both wondered why they weren't marrying each other. Daren looked at the beautiful wedding gown and grew sad as the bride within it walked away. He always knew that she would be a beautiful bride, however, he never imagined anyone marrying her other than himself. As "Here Comes the Bride" echoed through the hotel, reality finally hit Daren. He rubbed his chin with his right hand in deep thought and began walking toward the banquet hall.

When Butter approached the doors to the banquet hall, her father met her there. "Daddy, are you ready?"

"Baby-girl, you don't have to do this if you don't want to," her father said as he looked down to her with comforting eyes.

Butter acted as if she didn't hear his words. She hooked arms with him and the doors opened for him to walk her down the aisle.

CHAPTER 3

"So what's up with Rick?" Deniese asked Tasha as they sat down for their Friday night talk session. They couldn't wait for Shannon to arrive.

Tasha gave Deniese a look of disgust.

"What! What was that look for? You two are breaking up?" Deniese asked with wide eyes.

"No," Tasha frowned, "but we should."

"What's wrong? You two look happy together."

"Yeah, we're cool and everything, but his hands are nasty. You know he's a mechanic, right?"

"Yeah."

"Well, he comes over from work all oily and shit and got the nerve to be wanting to touch on me."

Deniese looked at her in disbelief. "He don't shower or nothing?"

"Yeah, he showers, but his fingernails still be outlined with oil. You know, they be all black around his cuticles. And he be wondering why I touch myself when we have foreplay. I'm like, 'because, motherfucka, I'll touch myself before I let your nasty-ass fingers touch my clit!' Fuck around and get an Amoco infection. Those are worse than yeast."

Deniese laughed with arched eyebrows. "Amoco infection? What in the world are you talking about?"

"If a bitch can catch AIDS, then I'm sure that we can catch some shit from oil and elbow grease."

"You crazy, Tasha!" Deniese yelled while giving her a high-five. Seconds later she got up to answer the knock at her door.

"Who is it?" Tasha yelled from the sofa. She looked up and found Shannon walking into the room.

"Alright," Shannon said in her party voice, " I got the Hennessy right here, so let's get this thing started." She was always in the mood for a good time. She had tons of positive energy and tons of friends.

Deniese followed Shannon into the room with a big smile. "Tasha, tell her what you just said about Rick."

"You tell her," Tasha replied with her famous frown.

"I can't tell it like you! Come on and tell her."

Tasha told the story, but Shannon didn't

think it was too funny. "Is that the only problem you have with Rick?" she said.

"That's enough," Tasha said with her eyes focused on Shannon. "It's bad enough that we can get yeast infections. What do you think I'll get from his oily fingers? I just told Deniese that I'm liable to catch an Amoco infection."

Shannon chuckled.

"Girl, please. Just keep touchin' yourself. At least Rick does take showers," Deniese said as she poured a glass of Hennessy. "Carlos was funky."

"You mean his breath?" asked Tasha.

"No."

"His underarms?" asked Shannon.

"No, his balls."

Tasha and Shannon laughed until tears came to their eyes, and watching them made Deniese laugh. "Y'all laughin', but that shit ain't hardly funny," Deniese added.

"Is that why he ain't around no more?" Shannon asked.

"Basically. He was mad because I wouldn't go down on him. Coming in here after running up and down the basketball court talking about he wants some head."

"Ugh! That's nasty," Shannon groaned. "I would have never expected that from Carlos. At least you don't have to worry about that, Tasha."

"Hell if I don't. Rick's balls, dick, and everything else smell like ass."

"That's nasty!" Shannon frowned. "I'm glad that I'm married and ain't gotta deal with such nonsense. You never told him that he was smelly? Why do they smell like that?"

"Men like him never learned to wipe themselves properly."

"I know that's right," said Deniese. "It's really not their dicks that stink. It's the part right behind their balls that separate the balls from the ass. It be smelling like straight funk. Sometimes it's cool for a while when you're down there, but the saliva, once it drips down there, activates the funk."

The women continued to drink and laugh until their glasses ran short of ice.

Tasha went on. "Men are always talking about sistahs don't go down. If they just washed their asses then we'd go down a lot more. I like sucking dick if he's clean."

"I know that's right," Deniese said. "How come they don't wash? Don't they know their asses stink? One time I made Carlos take a shower and he came into the room with his face smelling like ass. He had the nerve to dry off his body and then dry off his face last. I started calling him *Butt Face*."

The three women laughed and then laughed harder as they began their third round of drinks. Suddenly there was another knock on the door, and it startled Tasha and Shannon, but Deniese knew the unique knock. She went to the door and returned with Daren.

"What's up, ladies," he said as he attempted to hug the three women one by one.

He successfully hugged his *sister* Deniese and Shannon, but Tasha didn't welcome his embrace. She loved his chocolate-toned skin, athletic build, handsome face, and his bright white teeth. Like most women that met Daren, she also admired his nice hands, well-groomed facial hair, his bald head, and his seductive scent, but she would never admit to any of this.

"Daren, how come you don't wash your ass?" she asked with a straight face?

As Deniese and Shannon fell across the sofa with laughter, Tasha broke a small smile. Daren noticed the glasses sitting next to the Hennessy bottle and knew he was in for a wild debate from the women.

"I wash my ass. Don't tell me that y'all are in here talking about asses? Y'all ain't got nothin' else to do?"

"Don't change the subject," yelled Tasha. "Does your girlfriend suck your dick? And if she does, does she stay down there?"

"Which one?" yelled Deniese.

The three women laughed and gave high-fives to each other as they chanted, "Player! Player!"

Daren simply shook his head and smiled at Deniese. "You know what? I'm not even going to comment on that statement because y'all know I'm not hardly a player. But I do love gettin' head from my special friend."

"Special friend?" Tasha yelled. "You must be gettin' head from a man. Only gay men be talkin' that 'special friend' shit."

Daren continued to smirk at Tasha as he shook his head. "Y'all are silly as I don't know what. I ain't going there with y'all to-night. Y'all trippin' up in here."

"No, we really need a man's opinion because some of you men wonder why we don't like going down," Shannon explained. "The three of us are working on *The Sour Dick Theory* which states that you guys don't wipe well enough."

"It's more than that," Tasha rambled on. "They don't wash their asses good enough, either. The funk builds up day after day after day...."

Daren gave a faint smile as he ges-tured to Deniese that he didn't want the drink she was offering him.

"I'm glad that you came over," said Deniese as she walked toward her hallway. "I need your help with my bedpost. It's loose."

"Deniese be fucking up some beds. You know that big girls like it rough. That prob-ably came from you and Joe. Y'all always having rough sex."

"Fuck you, Tasha. I'm full-figured," Deniese yelled over her shoulder to the liv-ing room as she and Daren walked through the hallway. Once inside Deniese's room, she closed the door. "What's up, Daren?"

"Ain't nothin' up."

"Alright, I can see that I have to pull teeth tonight. Well, I know that I can't make you talk, but I just wanted to let you know that I'm your sister and I can tell when shit ain't right with you."

"Naw, everything's cool. What's wrong with your bed?"

"Dummy, ain't nothing wrong with it. I just wanted to talk to you in private. But what's been up? You ain't been returning my calls or anything for the past few weeks."

"I emailed you," Daren said smiling.

"I know. That means that you don't want to talk to me. You just drop a line and you're through. We normally talk all of the time. We ain't talked in weeks. I know something's going on, but that's your business."

"Everything's cool. Just got some things on my mind, that's all," Daren said still smiling.

"Alright. I'm still here whenever you want to talk," Deniese said walking to the door. "By the way, I have another friend for you to meet. She's real nice, too. I think y'all would make a cute couple. Never mind. You got some stuff going on with you right now. I'll introduce y'all when you get your stuff together. Come on in here so we can whip them in Spades. We're going to Boston their asses to death."

Although they played Spades for years, this was the first time Deniese and Daren ever lost to Shannon and Tasha. Daren renigged twice and cut his partner several times.

"In your face!" Tasha yelled. "Beating y'all is easier than playing *Uno*."

"Tell 'em, Tasha. We servin' them like they been doing us all of those times. It's payback tonight got-damnit!"

Deniese couldn't believe that they lost. "Daren, I don't know what's on your mind, but you need to get your shit together. I don't like losing, and now I gotta hear these fools brag until next time. Are you teaching school this year? Do you need some money?"

"I'm teaching, and no, I don't need any money."

"Well, if you ain't broke then it's some girl on your mind. Take care of it because you ain't yourself. You ain't talk trash to Tasha when you came in like you normally do, and you lost us the game. Go home and handle your shit!"

CHAPTER 4

Butter sat patiently waiting for her husband to return. It was her honeymoon, and the visions of how the night would be, which originated in her childhood, were flashing in and out of her mind. She thought about how she used to act it out with her Barbie and Ken dolls. One week in sunny Jamaica would be all that she would need to relax. It was bad enough that she had to wait seven weeks after her wedding for the honeymoon, but her boss, her son, and new stepdaughter made the seven weeks feel like a year. This time alone with her knight in shining armor was all that she needed.

She began to go over her mental checklist to be sure that everything was packed;

curling iron, soap, toothpaste, lingerie, scarves, lotion, alcohol, body oils, perfume, make-up kit, new lipstick, handcuffs, long feather, etc. She believed that she had everything. Now, after a hard day at work, all that she had to do was make sure that the kids were packed and ready. Butter's son, Billy, would be staying with *his* grandmother, while her stepdaughter would be staying with *her* mother. As Butter and the kids silently watched TV, they heard the family car pull up near the balcony door.

"Grab your bags and cut the television off," Butter commanded as she stood and grabbed her suitcase. "Your father is here."

"Yeah, Jasmine, *your* father is here," Billy said.

His statement went unnoticed by Jasmine, but his mother caught it and she sent him an icy stare. Billy's eyes retreated from Butter's and he turned the TV off, grabbed his duffel bag, and walked outside. As her husband came through the door, Butter rushed toward him and gave him a big hug.

"Welcome home, baby," she said as she got on her tippy-toes and planted a big kiss on his lips and hugged his wide, muscular frame. "The house is secure, our neighbors are going to collect our mail, and your mother-in-law is going to stop by to check on the house while we're gone."

"Tammy, look here, there was a slight mix-up with our vacation-honeymoon package, so we ain't going to be leaving today."

"What? So when are we going?"

"I don't know, yet. The minute they tell me I'm going to let you know."

Butter's husband then ran to the bedroom. She waited for him to return with an April Fools in August, but it never happened. Instead, he returned with his Allen Iverson jersey and his basketball shoes on.

"Where are you going?"

"I'll be back. Just going to play some ball."

"But we -"

Before she could finish her statement Donald had closed the door. She then heard the car engine roar. As she looked at her overstuffed suitcase, heated teardrops flooded her eyes. She immediately ran to her bedroom and locked the door. As she collapsed on the bed in disbelief, she scrambled to make sense of what just happened, but she couldn't.

It then dawned on her that she had never seen a plane ticket, an itinerary, nor reservations. But, then again, she never saw any of those things when she and Daren went somewhere. *Daren would never have done this*, she thought. *He always had everything taken care of*. She thought about Daren from time to time after the wedding, but never with so much focus and so much passion. He suddenly became a place of refuge for her saddened thoughts. Daren always took care of everything.

Butter then thought about calling her mother, but she decided against it. She wasn't in the mood for explaining. No, she wanted to pour her heart out and then hear the voice on the line verbally bash her husband, and her mother wouldn't do that. She decided on calling Robin. She didn't like her husband so she would give an earful. Butter dialed the number and waited.

"Robin speaking."

"Robin, guess what," Butter said in her crying voice.

"You ain't going on your honeymoon."

"How did you know?"

"Because I know you're with a sorry excuse for a man. What's his reason for canceling everything? You've been waiting two months for a honeymoon. I knew this was going to happen back when he said he wanted to hold off on having the honeymoon when you first got engaged; talking about he wanted to save for a house. I'm sorry for talking bad about him, but I don't like you being hurt."

"Thank you, girl. Talk on."

"I'm serious. You haven't cried like this since you were with Billy's father. Well, you did cry once or twice with Daren, but those incidents were your fault."

Butter began to laugh and cry at the same time.

"Where are the kids?" Robin asked.

"My husband took Billy to my mother's and his daughter to her mother's."

"Well, at least you two have a week off to spend together. I know some creative things that you can do together. They're really freaky ideas, too. I'm going to pick you up so we can go get some ice cream and -"

"Been there and done that with Daren," Butter interrupted.

"Now, girl," Robin corrected, "the ice cream is to cheer you up. I was going to suggest that we hit that homemade ice cream place down Georgetown and then you could pick up some things from the Sex Shop down there. Then you can whip it on him so good tonight that he'll be planning your honeymoon as you stroke him."

"I ain't going to see him tonight," Butter said as the tears reappeared and her feelings altered her speech. "H-h-h-h-he is out playing b-b-b-b-b-basketball and h-h-h-he always comes home late and sleepy."

"Mommy, are you crying?"

The sound of Billy's voice startled Butter. Her wishful thinking about her husband being considerate made her believe that he would have at least dropped the kids off as planned.

"Billy, Mommy's okay," Butter yelled while trying to speak clearly.

"I'm going to kill him for making you cry! Watch!"

"You ain't going to kill my daddy!" Jasmine responded.

"If he makes my mother cry again, I am!"

"No you ain't, neevuh. You too small."

"I'll get Loco to do it."

"No you won't, neevuh."

Butter would have normally disciplined the kids before they got so deep into such a heated argument. However, she felt weakened by the current circumstances of her postponed honeymoon. She didn't want to talk to the kids or look at them. She just wanted to remain in bed.

"Tamela? Tamela?" Robin called. "He didn't take the kids?" Robin took Butter's sobs as a no. "I'm on my way over there."

Robin rushed to Butter's apartment and took the kids to Butter's mother. She then went and picked up Butter and drove her to the ice cream shop as she had planned. They sat on the benches in front of the shop and talked about everything but Butter's predicament. Butter's phone began to ring.

"You're going to have to tell him how you feel eventually," Robin stated. "Marriage is about good communication. Just be nice when you tell him."

Butter frowned at Robin as she answered the phone. "Hello?"

"Tamela, your daughter says that she wants to go to her mother's house," said Butter's mother with a hint of sarcasm in her voice. "I ain't got time to be foolin' with this little girl."

"Okay, tell her -"

"Wait, there's more. Your son has decided that he wants to move back with me without you. What's going on?"

Butter was just beginning to relax with Robin and her ice cream, but her mother's call brought the stress right back. She felt that none of this would be happening if she were in sunny Jamaica. As the tears began to resurface in her eyes, Robin grabbed the phone and continued the conversation. As Robin talked with Butter's mother, she looked at Butter to notice her staring into space as her ice cream dripped down her hand. Robin gave her a couple of napkins and she wiped her hand. Seconds later, more ice cream dripped down her hand and Butter slowly wiped it away; never once did she lick her cone. Robin just shook her head and continued talking. Minutes later she was done.

"Tamela, everything's okay for now. Your mother said that your new daughter has to get used to her eventually. And she said she's going to talk to your son. And you know what? She knows about the honeymoon already. Your son told her that Donald was out playing basketball and you were home crying."

Butter stopped staring into space and her eyes began to wander.

"You know, I didn't even think about him telling, but I should have. He was very upset when he heard me crying."

"I know," added Robin. "He expressed himself quite thoroughly when I drove him and Jasmine over there. I tried talking to him, but I don't think my little boyfriend paid me any mind. He was upset."

"I think he's jealous that I have another man in my life."

"No," Robin disagreed. "He just doesn't like Donald. He never did if you recall."

Butter shook her head in slow agreement.

"Anyway, your mother went on to say that Donald asked her and your step-father for a loan."

"What!" Butter yelled.

"That's what your mother said."

"Robin, he has money! He works two jobs. Where is his money going?"

"I don't know. Don't ask me. He ain't my husband."

Butter sat in front of the TV, but she wasn't watching it. For the second time that day she was waiting for her husband to return. The first occasion she was overwhelmed with seductive fantasies. This occasion she was overwhelmed with pain, frustration, and disappointment. When she heard an unfamiliar engine approach she didn't pay it any mind. However, the key clicking, along with the doorknob turning, did get her attention.

"Hey, baby," said Donald as his huge, muscular frame walked into the living room. "Come on! Let's go."

Butter looked at Donald with confused eyes. On one hand, she was excited about going on her honeymoon. On the other hand, she questioned why he took her through so many emotions in one day. She also wondered why in the hell he asked her parents for a loan, and since they said no, where did he get the money for the honeymoon.

"I'll get my suitcase," Butter said as she slowly stood from the sofa.

"No, you don't need it. Let's just go. Hey, where are the kids?"

"Over my mother's. Why don't I need my bags?"

"Just come on, baby." Donald held the door open as Butter walked through it. In the parking place for his 1993 Honda Civic was a 2000 Expedition. The unfamiliar engine now made sense to Butter. "You like it?" Don asked.

"Did you buy it?"

"Yeah, I bought it. I ain't leasing."

"How much did it cost?" Butter asked while her heart began to beat frantically.

"I got a good deal on it."

"You said you got a good deal on our honeymoon."

"There you go. Look, let's go and have some fun. Just get in the truck. I'll explain all of that."

Butter couldn't wait to hear exactly what happened. As she opened the huge passenger door and attempted to get aboard, she found that it was a lost cause.

"Baby, let me help you," Donald laughed as he helped her up into the truck. His laughter was uncontrollable.

Butter closed the heavy door and put on her seatbelt. She was trying to stay upset, but Donald's laughter loosened her up against her will. She then began to stare in amazement at the size of the truck and all of the features on the dashboard. With her view overlooking the hoods of cars, she felt as if she was in control of the road. She felt so safe. They ended up at the BET Soundstage. Once they were seated and waiting on their food, Butter remembered what she was upset about.

"So, tell me what's going on?"

"Alright. Baby, I've been trying to get a new ride for a long time because that Civic isn't any good. I figured that this truck would be big enough for the entire family so we'll have enough space when we travel. It seats eight people with more than..."

Butter wanted her husband to get right to the honeymoon, but she waited patiently.

"...and after dealing with them for the past two weeks they finally found a company that would finance it, so here it is. I had to pay extra money for a down-payment because of my credit and I had to dip into the honeymoon savings account."

"How much is the car note?" Butter asked with boiling blood. She couldn't wait to go through the roof.

"Now, before you get mad, understand that the truck is for the family. You can drive it, too. I also found us a house. We're moving in two months, but the car note is $730. Look, we can always go on a honeymoon, and when we do, we will come back home to our own house and not that small apartment."

Butter couldn't believe her ears. Once again she was on an emotional roller coaster. No honeymoon – mad as hell, new house – happy. A $730 car note – furious as hell, family vehicle – happy again.

After eating, Donald drove Butter to Beltway Plaza to see the late movie. She always felt safe with her husband because of his size and stature, which almost equaled her father's. However, her first thought was how Daren had told her how he would never take her to Beltway Plaza's movie theatre at night because she deserved something classier. She always assumed that it was because Daren had a girlfriend that worked there or that he took other women there all of the time. After standing in line she understood what Daren meant.

Two guys were arguing in line behind them. As one accused the other of looking at him the wrong way, a fight broke out and the guy that was looking at the other the wrong way had his crew of four friends beat-down and stomp the accuser. This went on until two security guards came. Where Daren would have pulled Butter away, Donald stood and watched. Butter was shocked and disturbed by the violence she had witnessed. Once in the theatre, she was surprised that the noise level before the movie started didn't change once the movie began. She couldn't hear anything and she sure didn't feel safe anymore. She just wanted to go home and sleep the rest of the day away. She had had enough.

CHAPTER 5

O ver two months had passed since Butter's wedding and the summer was coming to an end. Chris and Steve stood in the hallway of Daren's apartment building in the midst of the humid weather. They had been knocking for minutes without an answer, but they knew that he was home because they could hear the music blasting. Since they arrived they heard the song "Brandy" by the O'JAYS play three times on repeat. They simply laughed and shook their heads because they knew Daren was playing the song for Butter.

Since her wedding, Daren only got with the fellas once a week to play ball. He no longer joined them for Dreamcast and Playstation night, cook-outs, fishing trips, or anything else they got together for. He also refused to answer his telephone on many occasions and now he wasn't answering the door. Chris and Steve were growing tired of knocking.

"Man, if your depressed-ass don't open this door!" Chris yelled.

"Yeah, you gonna be needin' a new door in a second if you don't hurry up!" Steve cosigned. "We gonna kick this one down!" After Steve kicked the door twice, Daren finally opened it.

"What the hell is wrong with -"

Before Daren could finish his statement, Steve and Chris bum-rushed the door and Steve tackled Daren. The two men wrestled, but Daren didn't put up much of a fight. As they did so, Chris went to the large CD player.

"Man, cut this shit off! Steve, look. Daren got the photo album out looking at Butter's old pictures." Daren and Steve laughed as Chris continued making observations. "He's in here reminiscing like I don't know what. You depressed, Daren?"

"No, I'm not depressed or anything. I'm just...Steve, get off of me...I just been busy thinking and stuff. Get off me."

"Well, we're tryin' to go to The Legend tonight so we can meet some nice ladies and dance. You tryin' to go?" Chris asked.

The crew hadn't been to a club in years, and back when they did they were all in relationships. However, Steve was single now and so was Daren.

"No, I'm not going to no club. I have work to do."

"Like what?" Chris asked.

"School starts next week and I have lesson plans and stuff to do."

"That's true," Steve said, "but you can do that tomorrow. Get dressed."

"Nope. I'm not messing with y'all like that."

"Don't let him up yet, Steve."

"Oh, I ain't. We got one more thing to do. Get the phone, Chris. It's right there," Steve said pointing to the end table.

Chris grabbed the phone and was about to dial when he made a discovery. "This fool got his ringer off! I thought only girls did that. Man, Daren, you are depressed. Let me hurry up and make this call. "Hello. Yeah, here he is. Talk to this fool!" Chris held the phone to Daren's ear while Steve continued holding him down.

Daren began to laugh uncontrollably as he heard the voice on the receiver. Steve then smiled and released his hold on Daren. It was D on the line, another member of the crew. D was the good guy; the voice of reason. He would never consider running a stop sign – not even at night. He would never jay walk, and he surely would not hang out with the crew unless it was a special occasion or an emergency.

"Look here, sir," D said calmly, "I need you to clap your hands."

"Clap my hands? For what?"

"Because you're single. What did Cameo say? Single guys clap your hands."

Daren laughed as the joke sunk in.

"I'm serious, sir," D continued. "See, you were single before, but never did you

live the *single life*. This is a code red situation. This is so serious that I'm even going
to go to the club with you guys. You know it
ain't no fun unless you're there, so get ready."

Daren knew that he had to go out with
the fellas because D never went. Just to see
D dance and watch all of the ladies swarm
him because of his muscles would be worth
going.

"Yeah, I'll be there," Daren said with a
smile. "Did somebody call George?"

"George is already coming and he's
bringing his brother Morris. So we straight,
right?"

"Yeah, we straight."

"Alright. Now put Chris back on the
phone real quick.

Steve reappeared from his trip to the
refrigerator as Daren held the phone out to
Chris. "Got the nerve to be around here all
sad about that girl. Ebony is who you need to
roll with. She is bangin'! Nice skin, sexy body
– and you're around here pressed over a
married woman."

"Steve, let me set the record straight,
I haven't been sad, depressed, or anything
like that. I've just been thinking...you know?
Cleansing myself so that I can reinvent myself. I'm not sure if I've been honest with
myself over the past couple of years. I don't
know if I've been true with my feelings and
true with my emotions."

Chris looked at Steve and for a brief
period there was a moment of silence. Then

Chris busted out laughing and so did Steve. "Daren done used the word emotions! That was as feminine as I don't know what. Wait till I tell D."

Steve and Chris continued laughing, but Daren simply smiled and made his way to the shower. As he washed himself he heard the door open.

"Man, won't y'all stop playin'? Damn." Daren just knew that they were going to try to turn off the hot water or throw something in the tub. The memory was still in his mind of the day he and Chris came back from fishing and they put a live fish in the tub while Steve was showering. They laughed for hours as Steve cursed at them and vowed to get revenge. Daren thought that his time to be joked on was upon him.

However, when Daren looked around the curtain he saw the door close and on the floor sat his CD player. A second later, Cameo's Single Life boomed from the speakers:

> *Every little thing you do*
> *makes me smile*
> *And if I had my way, baby*
> *I'd tie you up awhile*
> *I flipped through the pages*
> *one by one*
> *I don't want to get too serious*
> *I just like having fun*

Daren couldn't help but to groove to the music, but he took a second to lock the door just in case they thought of a joke to pull on him.

Thoughts of Butter were vivid in Daren's mind. He had accepted her taking that huge step without him and he wasn't sulking. Daren basically decided to work on himself personally. He felt that if he continued reading, exercising, working, and remaining busy, his mind would soon be clear of his lost love. Butter was in his every thought, but as the song commanded, "Single guys, clap your hands," Daren began to clap. Soap got into his eyes and he leaned into the shower stream, but not once did he stop clapping. It dawned on him that very second that D was right – he had never really lived the single life, and it was time that he did.

*   *   *

Daren and Chris were dancing with some women to Rick James' "Give It To Me Baby", while Steve, George, Morris, and D stood to the side. Steve was busy looking for a potential midnight playmate. The Legend was definitely jumping tonight.

"Thank you for the dance. Let me talk to you for a second," Daren said to the short, brown woman that looked like she dressed not to impress. She wore a pair of blue pants and a white turtleneck which had tiny teddy bears on it. Daren overlooked her outfit because he was open to making friends with anyone that had mental sense regardless of their fashion sense. He knew that the fashion police were ready to whip her ass and lock her up.

"No, that's okay. Bye." The woman dissed Daren and walked away.

Daren played it off and began to dance to the next song by himself.

"You gonna dance with me?"

"Of course," Daren said to the new woman that approached. "Come on over here."

The woman laughed and got into the groove. Daren didn't push up on that butt, he just played it from a distance. This woman wasn't too appealing to the eye with her odd body frame and super-saggy black blouse and skirt.

"I'm Lisa. Nice to meet you. And you are?"

"Daren."

"Daren, I just lost about 65 pounds so excuse the loose clothing."

"Oh yeah? That's an amazing accomplishment. You look good."

"Thank you," Lisa blushed. "It's going to get better. I lost the weight, now I have to tone up."

"If you lost 65 pounds I'm sure that you will continue to win your body back. You've come a long way."

"Thank you," Lisa said. She was overjoyed because of Daren's optimism and words of encouragement. Just then the music changed to TLC's "Red Light Special" and Lisa grew anxious. "I know everybody's leaving the dance floor, but this is my song. Can you dance with me just one more time?"

Daren wasn't one for rejecting simple requests. He gently, but securely, grabbed her around her waist and pulled her to him.

"Dag," Lisa whispered. "Your chest feels like a brick wall." She then placed her left hand on his right pectoral muscle and held it for the duration of the song while her right hand held his back. When the song ended she did not want to let go. "Daryl?"

"Daren."

"Sorry about that, but Daren, I would like to dance with you some more just like that. You really know how to hold a woman. Let me write my number down so you can call me." Lisa pulled Daren off of the dance floor and got a pen and paper from her girlfriend.

"Girl, his chest is so hard and muscular," Lisa chimed.

"His friend over there with the big, cute nose has the real muscles. Look how big he is," the friend said as she pointed to D.

"He has a girlfriend," Daren informed.

"So. He wouldn't want me because I'm too old to be his girlfriend. Right, Lisa?" Lisa looked towards the ground in non-agreement. "I just want to teach him a thing or two. Introduce us, please."

Daren respected D's relationship with his girlfriend, and he knew that D would be able to handle the situation. He introduced the two and suddenly the introduction of Maze and Frankie Beverly's "Before I Let Go" came on. Everyone rushed the dance floor and the woman grabbed D's hand and pulled him in the same direction. D, being the nice guy that he is, went with her with a puzzled expression on his face. Daren went back to the crew to chill.

"What's up with that chic?" Steve asked.

"Nothing. Just dancing. She gave me her number."

"How old is she? She got to be about 40 or 45. They say that there's always an old guy in the club, but there's always an old lady, too."

"That's right," Chris added, "and that old lady can get fucked, too." He and Daren nodded in unison and shook hands.

"Look at D! Look!" George yelled.

D was getting busy on the dance floor as the woman Daren introduced to him draped herself all over D and stared at him through her bifocals while rubbing his bald head. When the song went off D walked over to the fellas. "Y'all see something funny?" D said with a sarcastic attitude. "Look at this," he said as he held up a small piece of paper that read: Peggy AKA Peggy-lady 301-555-7638. "Peggy-lady?" D continued. "Peggy-lady? You know how old she is? She's 46!"

"For real?" Daren asked.

"Yeah."

"Fuck her," Chris said. "That's some ripe, 46-year-old pussy! You need to just fuck her good."

D just looked at Chris like he was crazy and then looked back to Daren. "Her friend, the one you were dancing with, is 48."

"She told you all that?" Morris asked.

"Her name is Peggy-lady, what do you think?" D said and the fellas went crazy with laughter. "She sounds like a talker, doesn't she? She has a son that's 29. He's older than me! Man, I'm going home. I don't need to be out here."

Chris looked at D with a disgusted look. "That's about your age, right? Stop acting like a lil' chump. D can bone!"

At that very second, Peggy-lady approached the crew. "D, you're going to call me, ain't you? Come on and walk me to my car. You're all big and strong with your cute nose. You can protect my friend and me."

"Yeah," Morris said. "Go ahead and protect her, Muscles."

Daren slowly walked away from the group so that Lisa would not ask him to walk with them. With Daren gone, D made Chris go with him. As Daren made his way through the crowd to the bar, the woman that dissed him, with the teddy-bear turtleneck, tapped his shoulder.

"Hi. I'm Mikala. Here's my card. Call me sometime so we can talk."

Daren wondered what prompted Mikala's approach. She didn't want to talk when he asked, but now she wants to. He told her his name, accepted her card, and proceeded to walk away when Steve came over.

"Come on, man, we rollin'. George and Morris already left. Chris and D are waiting on you."

Daren followed Steve to D's car and they headed out.

D started talking once they hit the road. "Man, I don't know about you guys, but I'm scared."

"Scared of what? You ain't drunk. You only had two drinks," Chris went on. "It takes about seven bonecrushers and four long island iced teas just to make your muscle-bound-ass catch a buzz."

"That was funny, sir. No, I'm not talking about being drunk. I'm talking about a species of animal known as Peggy-lady. Chris, you know what I'm talking about."

"You mean at the car just now? Steve and Daren, y'all missed it. Peggy-lady felt D on the ass and kissed his head. Then she told him that he resembled her first husband, and said that she bets that he makes good love and to call her."

"Uh-huh," D shook his head up and down making sure he kept his eyes on the road. "That mess is crazy! I'm not going out with y'all for a long time. I don't care how depressed Daren gets. I'm scared. Daren, you can call her friend, but I'm not calling Peggy-lady."

"Oh yeah," Steve interrupted, "you just got another woman's phone number, didn't you? That chick with the Garanimals on."

The entire car broke out with laughter.

"Hell yeah," Chris said. "I remember Garanimals way back in the 70's. They made shirts with hippos and rabbits and shit. People with Gator shirts would cut you up if you wore Garanimals. And Daren just got a woman's number that wears that shit in the year 2000? We gonna cut his ass up!"

"You gonna call her? What's her name?" Steve asked.

"Her name is Mikala."

"She gave you a card? Let me see it." Steve held it to the window so that he could read it clearly. "Mikala or Aunt Mike? What kind of shit is this?" Steve began laughing and Daren snatched the card and read it to himself, *Mikala or Aunt Mike 703-555....* "Yup, that's what it says. It does say Aunt Mike."

Chris began joking. "I thought Steve was just trying to be funny. You better check her Adam's apple and her hands and feet. Aunt Mike? That shit is worse than Peggy-lady."

They went on joking about the entire club and everything that went down. Butter jumped back into Daren's mind and, although she was in the front, she now had Lisa and Aunt Mike as background singers. For three hours at the club Daren actually didn't think about Butter at all.

"Forget all of that," D said. "I'm scared. I don't care if Peggy-lady looked like Halle Berry or Vivica Fox. I'm happy in my relationship with my sweetheart. I can't wait to tell her about Peggy-lady. I feel sorry for anyone that's single. You guys may be able to handle it, but I know that I couldn't handle being single these days."

CHAPTER 6

Butter lay in bed wishing she had a warm body next to her and hoping her husband would come home. While she read Michael Baisden's *The Maintenance Man*, her mind began to drift away with thoughts of being comforted by another man. She then determined that her cheating thoughts were being generated by the book she was reading, so she put it down in exchange for something smoother. She enjoyed books by Baisden and Travis Hunter because of their high level of entertainment and sexual content, but she couldn't handle them while suffering from sexual deprivation. She picked up *Not With My Son* by Hope C. Clarke, knowing it would get her through the night.

The sound of the front door unlocking snapped her out of the world the author created for her. Days ago she would run to the front door and greet her husband, but as his days out with the guys continued and his return time became later and later, she walked to the door with less fervor.

"Hey, Tamela, you still up?" Her husband asked as he began to undress at the front door. Butter gave him a soft kiss with thoughts of finally making love to him. Trying to suppress her anxiety, Butter double checked the stove to make sure everything was off, then she pranced to the bathroom to make sure her body was fresh. After a splash of Listerine to her mouth and a quick wipe-down of her vagina, she rushed to the bedroom and dabbled a few drops of Romance to the essential places. She then lit a candle and jumped in bed. This was the night she had been waiting for, and after hearing no sign of her husband, she decided that being patient a little longer would not hurt.

After mentally playing what she wanted to take place several times in her mind, and getting herself worked up, she decided to hell with patience and went to see about her husband. She had waited for him over fifteen minutes, and another minute, in addition to how long it had been since their last episode between the sheets, was too long.

Upon returning to the living room she found her husband laid out on the sofa sound asleep.

*   *   *

As I step out of the doors of P.G. Plaza, the sun beamed down with a vengeance. Being in this shopping mall for the past hour made me forget just how hot it was out here. Hearing a few feminine voices behind me, I catch the door and hold it for the two 30ish women and the two children with them.

"Thank you," says the short, light skin, thick woman as her eyes meet mine for a brief moment. "A real gentleman."

"No problem, sis," I respond as I begin walking to my car. Evidently their car is in the same area because it's almost as if I'm following them. Just then the women glance back and look at me, whisper to one another, and then smile. We arrive at their car and as I walk past, the same woman that spoke to me earlier says, "Bye." She must be looking at my arms and shoulders in this wife-beater that I'm wearing. I look back and give her an over the shoulder smile and walk two spaces to my car.

While driving I see the flirtatious woman's car in front of me. I simply keep driving and drift away into the music blasting from my radio. A mile or so later I notice that she's still driving in front of me as if she knows where I'm going. Maybe it's destiny that we meet. I pass her car, wave at her while blowing my horn, and make a right off of Kenilworth Avenue onto Goodluck Road. She drives through the light and holds up one finger. I quickly pull into a church parking lot just to see if that finger was her index finger telling me to wait a minute. I hope it wasn't her middle finger telling me to fuck off.

Yup, here she comes. She parks in front of me and turns her car off. I immediately look into the rearview to make sure my nose is clean and my look is right before I get out and approach her car.

"Hey, how are you doing?" I say with less than flirtatious eyes. I can't flirt with kids around. Ain't nothing cool about that.

"I'm fine and I'm glad that you're doing well. You went to H.D. Woodson with me. Didn't you?" she asks with a heavy country accent.

"No, I didn't go to -"

"Yes you did," the woman suggested as she rolled her eyes to the backseat where the children were.

"Oh yeah," I say finally catching on. "You did go to Woodson with me. How have you been?"

Just then the little boy stood up and grabbed onto the driver's headrest and peeked his head around. "Mommy, you went to school with that man?"

"Yes, sweetheart, and I haven't seen him in a long time." She then turned away from her son's direction and found my eyes. "You know that I forgot your name..."

"Daren."

"Yes. I know you forgot my name, Daren. It's Rita."

After introducing me to her best friend and her son and young daughter, she wrote down her phone number. Getting back into my car I assume she wears at least a 38DD. Those things were damn near sitting on the steering wheel. I'll bet she weighs about a hundred and eighty pounds. She looks so sweet. Damn, just days ago I could only think about Butter. Now I have the woman with the Garanimals, the baggy woman, and this sweet young lady with the country voice.

*   *   *

It's the first day of school and I am the happiest man on earth. I don't know if my jubilation is because I finally get to see all of my students or because this horrid summer is finally over. I can't believe Butter got married. Anyway, I have a host of new women, I have today's lesson planned for my intelligent fourth graders, and I'm ready to get this school year started on the right foot.

After greeting all of the children at the door, I tell them to use the locker with their name on it. Afterwards they must find their assigned seat, take out their paper, and complete the first assignment. I give them a short and simple math assignment just to loosen the cobwebs in their minds from the long summer break. Then they are to write three paragraphs about what career they want to pursue when they get older. This not only loosens their minds, but it displays their writing skills, level of English, and their speaking skills. But more importantly, it tells me about their personalities. Thirty minutes into class and we've already checked the math warm-up and heard several oral presentations. Everything is going well – so far, so good.

"Stephen Graham, your turn, son." I call all of my male students *son*.

"I want to do two different careers when I become an adult. The first career is an optometrist because I like science and I like helping others. People everywhere need glasses so I'll help them by putting the medicine in the lenses. Optometrists make a lot of money, too, and I can use it to help my family move out of Southeast. I would also like to work on cars because all of my life my uncles have worked on cars and I like to watch and help them. I like..."

Now this little boy has it together. I like his way of thinking and how articulate he is. Upon finishing his speech we all clap and I congratulate him on a job well done. "Angela Thompson, you're next, sweetie." A nice girl with a tall build and thin frame stands and walks to the front of the room with paper in hand. She looks so studious. I have the bomb class this year!

"When I grow up I want to be a police lady," Angela says and raises her eyes up to look at me and her fellow students. I hope that she doesn't think she's done after that one sentence.

"That's good, Angela," I say trying to urge her on. "You want to be a policewoman so you can clean up Wheeler Road and the other streets of Southeast?"

"No, I just wanna bust a cap in somebody's ass."

I can't believe what I just heard. While half of the class laughs and the other half sits with their eyes bugging out with hands over their mouths, I tell Angela to sit next to me. After her statement she hasn't cracked a smile at all. Her expression is a serious one. While the next person presents, I ask Angela to explain herself to me.

"For real, Mr. Brown. All the police do around here is bust caps in people's -"

I cut her off and explain to her what words are not appropriate to use in class. I then have to explain what appropriate means. I can tell that this is going to be a very long year.

It's finally Friday and I have so much stress to release. I am up in Zanzibar on the Waterfront pouring my heart out to Chris and Steve and making them laugh.

"Man, those kids have drove me crazy already. Angela is no joke at all. She has been on earth before. I'm serious. She can't be nine-years-old because she knows too much. I think the child is 16 at the least. And along with her grown-ass I have three special education kids that require primary attention. The worst one is Brandon. He will damn near whip all these kids' asses. He's almost as tall as me. It's hard to teach the other 23 kids because his bad-ass is always starting a fight with somebody."

After telling them about Angela and why she wanted to be a policewoman, they damn near died from laughter. They just knew I was lying. As we continued to talk and laugh, a woman stood near us and stared at me. At first I didn't pay her any attention, but after she stood there another minute or two I looked at her.

"Raquel?" I say finally recognizing the woman. "Damn, what a surprise. How have you been? Why didn't you say something?" She was my sixth grade girlfriend and she looks really good.

"I didn't think you would remember me and I didn't want to embarrass myself. I see you are still cutting up and having a good time."

She's qualified for the cover of Essence Magazine. Her skin is a creamy, honey-coated chocolate tone, eyes are beautiful, thick, sexy lips, toned body, and she's probably about 5'10" with heels. After introducing her to the crew, talking to her, and getting our dance on, it's time to roll. I don't bother to give her my number because she's married. I just hurry to catch up with my crew who's meeting me by the main entrance downstairs. Before I hit the stairs I come across a lovely woman that looks like a fish out of water.

"What are you doing here?" I ask.

"Excuse me? Do I know you?" she says as if she isn't to be spoken to.

"You really need to know me. I'm glad I came across you before leaving. I asked you that because you don't look like the type to be here."

"And how do I look?" she asks in a sophisticated tone that coincides with her style of dress.

"You look a lot like me. We both resemble fish out of water or hookers and pimps in church." As she smiles I continue. "We need to talk this week so by next Friday we can be in a place more conducive to our personalities." With those words she hands me her card.

"I'm Marcy, and I appreciate your realness. And you are?"

"Daren, and I appreciate your time and your eye contact. I'll call you soon," I say as I shake her hand and make my way down the stairs. She appreciates how real I am because that's the only way I know how to be. I now have the Garanimal chick, the baggy one, Country, and Marcy in my mix. I even got to see my sixth grade love. Things are looking good. These are more than enough for me to handle.

CHAPTER 7

"Hello," came her country voice over the receiver.

"And how are you doing?"

"I'm doin' well. And yourself?"

"I'm cool. Do you know who you're talking to?" I ask.

"I sure don't, but it'd be nice if you help me," she says with her country accent. It's funny how she pronounces certain words.

"This is Daren."

"Really? I didn't think you would actually call."

"Why not?"

"Men'll do that – take your number and not call. But I'm glad you did."

"Is that right?" I ask flirtatiously.

"That's right."

"So where are you from with that cute, country accent?"

"West Virginia."

"Damn, you're the only black person I've met from there. What brings you to P.G. County?"

"Met my ex-husband, moved out here, got married, got divorced, now it's me and my little boy and girl."

"That sums it all up. But tell me this, what is it that you're looking for? A boyfriend, sex partner, husband?"

"Hmmm...I'm looking to get married again. I grew up with both parents in the home and I want my kids to have the same luxury. Besides, nothing beats having a man around the house. Isn't everybody looking to get married?"

I ain't marrying nobody! Isn't everybody looking to get married? How naive can this woman be? "How soon are you trying to get married?"

"The minute I find the right person. I'll be forty in six years."

That's very honest of her. I respect that, but it ain't for me right now. Two kids, a structured home, and she's thirty-four? I'm trying to have two kids in about five years and she'll be about forty then. I know she ain't gonna wanna have two more pregnancies at that age. And I damn sure ain't trying to get married now.

"Let me be straight-up with you, I'm not looking to get married for another five years or so. You sound like a nice woman and I hope that you find what you're looking for.

I know there is someone out there suitable for that role that you're looking to be filled."

"Thanks for warning me. Now we won't waste each other's time."

"I don't think we will. You can still keep me around, right?"

"I can't do that. You're cute and very handsome, but I need someone for the long haul. Someone marriage-minded. I've been without a man, or the comfort of a man, for almost eighteen months."

"Well, are your needs being met? Are you being satisfied emotionally and pleased sexually?"

"No, but -"

"Do you like pizza?" I ask calmly after cutting her off.

"I love pizza, but what does that have to do with anything?"

"Well, one day you're going to have steak every night. There will be a nice filet mignon there to satisfy your appetite. But, until then, I'm willing to deliver a pizza to your door whenever you get a little hungry."

There is a brief moment of silence, but finally she speaks. "I've never had a relationship like that before. Let me get back to work. It's been nice talking to you."

"Okay, love. Have a nice afternoon." Dag, she seems really sweet. It would have been nice to get to know her. Delivering pizza? Where in the world did I get that analogy from?

*   *   *

I couldn't wait to call Marcy after another stressful day with my fourth graders.
Marcy is the woman that I met on my way
out of the club – the woman that looked like
she didn't belong in that setting. I had to
talk to somebody and I'd usually talk to Robin,
but Ebony told me that Robin is still upset
because of me and Ebony's escapade. I definitely ain't calling Garanimals or the Baggy
Lady, and Country ain't never call me so I
guess I can scratch her off of my list.

"Oh, you're just a baby," Marcy says
after I tell her my age.

"You think so?"

"Yes. You're fine, but just a little too
young for me. I can hook you up with my
daughter since you have such a good head
on your shoulders. She's twenty-one and in
her last year of undergrad at Florida A&M."

"What? She's a Rattler?" I ask trying to
hide my disappointment. How is she going
to say I'm too young? Well, she has an adult
child so I assume she's at least thirty-eight
or thirty-nine. She needs to understand that
I prefer older women?

"Daren, what do you know about FAMU?"

For the next three hours Marcy and I
discuss everything from Billie Holiday and
HTML, to the Harlem Renaissance, Bill Clinton,
and George W. Bush. It seems as if we left
no subject unturned, and I can tell that she
enjoyed it.

"You know something, Daren? I like you. I'm going to have to keep you for myself. Not only are you smart, but you're also a good listener. You might be too old for my daughter. Besides, I don't know if my daughter can handle being turned out at such a young age."

I'm amused at her statements. "Turned out? Where did you get that from?"

"A woman's intuition. A woman knows if the dick is good. Plus, you're confident and attentive. We've brushed over the topic of sex and not once did you jump on it or brag on yourself; most men would have. I can tell that you'll pay close attention to my body. So, are you okay with being with me?"

"Sounds good to me. I'm okay with it. That's what I wanted from the start."

"You're not intimidated by a forty-year-old woman, Daren?"

"Forty-years-young," I correct her.

"That's good. You make a woman my age feel good with compliments like that. Keep them up."

"I'm just speaking the truth. They say life starts at 40. If that's the case, then you're just being born."

"And, Daren, that would mean you're stuck up in the fallopian tubes somewhere, huh?"

"That's right, sweetie."

"You're too funny," Marcy says, then she gets serious on me. "Well, before I become your sweetie, let's get a few things straight.

Number one, do you have A.I.D.S. or any sexually transmitted diseases?"

"No," I respond.

"Have you been tested?"

"Yes, five months ago."

"Great! I want to see the results if you don't mind. I'm not trying to offend you, but a woman needs to know these things. Please bring the results when we go out this week."

I didn't know we were going to be going out so soon. "No, I respect you asking me. I'd like to see your results, too. Anything else you want to ask?"

"No, but I do have something to explain to you."

"I'm listening, sweetie."

"I'm 40 years-old. I've been married for 17 years, had the family, a house with a white picket fence, and a dog. I'm separated from my husband, I own a house and a condo, I have five cars and I make $85,000 a year after taxes, and that's not including overtime and special projects. I have done all that you wish to do and probably forgotten more than you have ever learned. What I'm saying to you is this, there is nothing that you can do for me that I can't do for myself. But, if you fuck me the way I want to be fucked and lick my pussy the way I want it licked, I'll make sure that you have everything your heart desires."

"Is that right?" I ask astonished at her honesty.

"That's right. When I come a lot, I lose my mind. You make me come hard and I'll give you my credit card to go shopping for yourself while I rest. I have a $150,000 limit with a zero balance. How much is yours?"

"Mine is about $13,000."

"That's a nice limit for your age."

"No, sweetie, I owe $13,000. My limit is $12,000."

Marcy begins a deep, seductive laugh that really sounds sexy. "Daren, you say you're a history major, right?"

"That's right."

"Well, you can do some freelance research for my firm and make some real money. I can help you make that $13,000 disappear like that," and she clicks her fingers. "Daren, you'll mess around and get rich from just being around me if you play your cards right. The research that you can do part-time with my firm will probably pay you more than your full-time job – and this job is stress-free."

Now what in the world have I stumbled into? I've met a woman that is not only sexy, but will put me on easy street. Marcy and I finally get off of the phone after over three hours of midday conversation. I simply sit and try to remember if my test results are in my file cabinet or with my business papers. The phone rings again and I'm wondering if it's Marcy wanting to see me tonight since it's Friday. That would be better than waiting two more days.

"Hello?"

"I sure would like some pizza."

It's Country! Now that's what I'm talking about. "I have lots of pizza, sweetie. What's your address?"

CHAPTER 8

Getting out of my car I can't help but to inhale dust from the construction that seemed to have taken place earlier. Country's house is at the end of a developed block of new town homes. To the right of her house are half-developed homes, building supplies, and trucks, surrounded by mounds of dirt.

Walking through the door I immediately give Country a big hug. She's on the thick side so I squeeze her a little.

"You look nice," I compliment and take her hand.

"You think so? That's sweet. Are you hungry?" she says while leading me from the foyer up into the dinning room.

As I begin to answer, the aroma of several dishes of soul food tell me all that I need to know. "What's that smell?"

"Nuttin' but some roasted chicken, sweet potatoes, string beans, and macaroni and cheese. Now go wash up and I'll get your plate ready. The powder room is right there on your left. What do you want to eat?" she asks as she walks into the kitchen.

"I want a lot of everything. Shoot, I don't shy away from food because I like to eat. And if you want me to eat you just hop your pretty self up on that plate." At my flirtatious words, Country looks over her shoulder and smiles.

I quickly wash my hands and face and get a good look at myself in the mirror. I love the confidence in my eyes and I love the way I look. I know I'm going to have some fun tonight with this sweet woman. I suddenly hear soft jazz music echoing through the house. Walking out of the powder room I find myself in complete darkness with a dim light illuminating from the deck in the backyard. I carefully walk through the darkness towards the light and close the screen door behind me. I sit in the chair in front of a huge plate of food, and I am in awe of how delicious it looks. Reaching for the fork I look at Country and begin eating.

"You're not eating?" I ask.

"No, I ate somethin' earlier today. I'm on a diet anyway."

Looking at her face I notice her skin and the thick layer of make-up caked on it. She looks like she's on her way to a photo shoot. Her short and stocky frame is burdened by huge breasts. You can't pay me to believe those aren't triple-D cups. Her eyes are squinty at the corners and her skin is a light banana shade. I reach across the table with my left hand and hold her right hand.

"Country, this food is good! Baby, you can really cook." Seeing my food disappear actually bothers me because I don't want my oral pleasure to end. "Damn, this is good. Why are you single again?"

"That's what everyone says that eats my food. I had a husband, but he loved another more than me."

"Oh, another woman or two?"

"No, crack. He loved crack more than he loved my cookin'."

"For real?"

"Yes, and all this started right before our second child was born. Once I found out he was smokin' crack and running the streets, I immediately got the kids and left. I agree with standing by my husband, but crack ain't a habit that you just break."

"And it can destroy a family. So how is he now?" I ask nonchalantly.

"He's doing better. He is engaged to a white woman now. The kids see him twice a month. He knows that whenever he's strung out he won't get to see his kids until he's clean again. Speakin' of clean, look at your plate. You want some more?"

"Baby, if I eat any more I won't be able to move." Country gets up and takes my plate and glass into the kitchen. I take the candle off of the table and go into the living room. There's nothing but a television in here and that doesn't have a cable box or a thick, black wire going into the wall. Damn, there goes watching any sports after I put Country to sleep. Just then I hear a little commotion and I look to find this triple-D woman carrying an air mattress. "Let me help you with that," and I take the half that she's dragging. We both lay it down and begin putting on the sheets.

"That was nice of you, Daren."

"What? Helping out?"

"No, Daren. I'm talkin' 'bout how you didn't just grab it from me. You helped me instead of just takin' over. That lets me know you're a good partner."

I now notice that Country has changed into a tight, dark green and black bustier that has a chiffon robe, which is also black. Her breasts are sitting up and out like two huge melons. She then begins telling me that the kids' rooms are finally furnished, but all that she has is a TV and air mattress. She left all of her belongings with her ex-husband, that goes for what was left of them. He had pawned or sold most of the living room, bedroom, and den. She explained that scenario as well as all of the pictures on the walls of her kids and her mother.

"I've only been here for three weeks so there's no furniture yet. I also have no cable. Sorry."

Now that I am concentrating on her she seems so nervous. I can tell that she wants me, but she doesn't want to make the first move. Now that my food has settled, I can put some work in. Shit, as good as her cooking is, I'm going to try to give it to her real good. I sit up from briefly laying on my side and look straight into her eyes as she sits Indian-style.

"Baby, you think I'd be in the presence of such a pretty woman as you and watch TV?" I slowly lean toward her and softly place my left hand on the side of her face. "Come here, baby. I have a special delivery for you."

Our lips meet and I begin to kiss her with smooth, long kisses. I won't dare give her short, quick kisses because I plan on giving her the long dick. Short kisses and short dick are for quickies, but since she has on this lingerie piece and we're by candlelight, then long kisses and long dick it is. Squeezing her makes me realize that her lingerie is actually hiding a fancy girdle, which is restraining her stomach. No wonder she didn't want to eat with me. Nevertheless, I continue kissing, squeezing, and touching while simultaneously taking her robe off. Country then lowers the top of her bustier and reveals the largest breasts I've ever seen.

I never imagined that breasts could be larger than Angel's. I know that I have to orally make love to them, but I am a little hesitant like women tell me they are when they are about to go down on a large man. I immediately flashback to the day of July 25. That was the day that Angel and I lost our virginity to each other...

After inserting myself and realizing that I was actually in an authentic vagina, I couldn't feel anything but bliss. After working my ass and hips in all of the stroking motions that I viewed on Anne Sprinkles, Taboo I and II, Mobile Home Girls, and any other X-rated video that I got my hands on, I decided to roll over and let Angel get on top.

For ten seconds she squirmed, but nothing was really happening – no stroking, pumping, or anything. Sitting still she lay on top of me and before I could take a deep breath, her 40EEs were smothering my face. I seen my life flash before my eyes as my breathing was cut short by two huge breasts.

Ironically, I began to squirm, which propelled her to squirm with me. I then grabbed her and swung her to the side and heard myself take a deep breath as I felt my heart racing. Happy to have fresh air, I got back between Angel's legs and long stroked her until cum exploded from my dick into the condom. It was that day that I not only experienced "vagina," but it was also the day I learned how big breasts can be very dangerous.

"Daren, is everything okay?" Country asks.

"Everything is fine, baby. Your breasts are so pretty and soft." I begin to kiss, lick, and suck on them to her delight. She then stops my hands as I attempt to take her girdle off. Instead, she puts my hand between her legs to which I unsnap the button and reveal her vagina. This woman is hot and ready so I reach for a condom and go to work. It's a little tight, but very willing because it strokes and pumps with me. I then feel her pumping harder so I begin to pump harder, and I realize that she has stopped, but I continue. I open her legs wider, put them up, out, around, and put each on one side of my body then the other side. I continue to shuffle them into different positions as I pump harder and harder. As she screams with delight, I rock her back on her neck and shoulder blades and try my best to imitate the movements of a Texas oil drill slamming down and up, down and up. I begin to come and then I release the position and her back comes crashing down to the mattress.

"I ain't neva! Oh! I ain't neva! That was the best! I ain't neva had it like that." The words panted out of her mouth like she just ran a race. All that I could hear after every word was her heavy breathing. "Oh my goodness! You delivered in so many different ways. I ain't neva felt so good or been done so well."

I immediately get up and hit the bathroom.

"The towel set on the counter is yours," she whispers. I wash myself and then hit the kitchen to get more of this woman's good cooking. As I return to the living room, all that I hear is her snoring. With no cable and bad reception, I look at all of the six video-tapes sitting on the VCR. Four Disney movies, A Barney tape, and Sparkle. Irene Cara it will be. I pop in Sparkle and push play. I turn the volume up just enough to drown out Country's snoring.

CHAPTER 9

W hen Butter heard the truck pulling up at 3:00 in the morning, she rushed to the bathroom to quickly freshen up. She had done this several nights a week only to be disappointed by her husband's lack of interest in her sexually. She pondered the reasons, thought of every angle that could have him uninterested in her, and even stared at herself in the mirror to see if her appearance had changed much since they met. Nothing had changed in her eyes, and Robin's words of encouragement made her more convinced. However, that still didn't stop her from changing her hairstyle and buying new clothes, which included a new outfit, shoes, and lingerie. Donald didn't comment on her new outfit that morning, but she would make him notice her lingerie tonight. She would demand his complete attention.

It seemed like every night that he came in late, he would undress in the living room and go to sleep on the sofa. She would peek out of the bedroom only to see the blue glare from the television and she would return to bed knowing that he wouldn't be there with her to keep her warm and snug. It hadn't been six months of marriage, but Butter felt like it was over already. The bills were getting paid, but she wasn't being loved or made love to. She couldn't imagine living 40 or 50 years neglected. She loved how her husband towered over her in size and stature. He was so tall, strong, and muscular. His weight laid so heavy when he was on top of her and she loved it. But more than that, she loved how it felt riding him – his huge frame made her feel like she was riding a horse. Yes, being a bouncer and working security at the club had him coming in early in the morning, but it would be well worth the wait if the loving was good.

Butter snapped out of her daze after realizing there was no noise coming from the living room. She immediately began to walk to the living room where she knew she would step over Donald's clothes only to see him sprawled out on the sofa. She walked softly through the hallway, and the blue glare from the television revealed the pile of clothes, proving that she knew her husband's habits of undressing at the door very well. However, the closer she got to the living room, the louder an odd sound became. She couldn't believe that her Donald was sitting on the sofa playing his video game.

"What are you doing? I thought you were in here sleep," Butter said with a disgusted expression that totally contradicted her red lingerie and sweet smell of Victoria's Love Spell. That used to be the scent that drove Donald crazy.

"I am tired. Shit, I was working at that club all night."

Butter waited a few seconds to make sure he was done explaining. Sure enough he was done, but he hadn't explained a thing in her eyes.

"Are you coming to bed?"

"Yeah, I'll be in there. You missed me?" Donald asked while finally turning his eyes to her. She loved the attention and softened her expression upon his last statement. "Come on and sit down here with me."

As Butter snuggled under her husband's massive arms she felt loved and protected. She felt like a child as she gripped his hard biceps. "I see you've been working out," she said trying to focus her eyes on him. It was hard for her to see without her glasses and the darkness of the room only made it harder. "So am I finally going to get to see your sexy body over top of me and feel you inside of me?"

"What do you mean finally?" Donald said without taking his attention from the game he was playing. "I'm just unwinding. I had a rough night because two big dudes got into a fight. I threw both of their asses out of the club by myself."

Butter turned her body toward him with great concern. "Are you okay?"

"I'm alright. My nerves are just up, that's all. Might get wild like an animal if I had sex with you and I'd rather be in the mood rather than scare you off." Donald was becoming agitated by his wife's presence. All of these nights she assumed that he was sleep were just fine with him. In all actuality, nine out of ten times he would be playing his video game as opposed to sleeping. He just wished she would go back to bed, but Butter had other ideas.

"Umph," she moaned with a seductive smile. "You'd be an animal, huh? That might be what I need – some wild sex." She then cuddled under his arms again and began stroking between his legs.

"Tamela! Stop! You're going to mess up my game!" He closed his legs escaping her grasp.

"Okay, I guess I'll go to bed all alone while you spend another night in here." She stood and began walking away. "It hasn't been but around six months and you're already tired of me. Is this marriage going to last?"

Because of Butter's talking Donald lost his concentration and the game ended. Normally he can play in peace because Butter doesn't hear him come in late, or she doesn't come out of the room because she thinks he's sleep, but not tonight. Concluding that she would probably distract him further, and also wanting to keep the peace in the home, Donald decided to give Butter what she wanted and continue playing his Playstation 2 after he got his nut.

"Tamela, come here."

"What?"

"Just come here and sit down with me."

Butter sighed, but sat next to him. As he began touching and rubbing on her she instantly became aroused. With her eyes closed, she began to breathe rapidly because she was finally going to feel what she had been waiting for – a stiff dick between her legs. Donald then got on top of Butter and started kissing on her neck. She felt bliss as his body weighed down on hers and his kisses sprinkled her neck. Suddenly there was a loud sound in the room and Butter's eyes shot open.

"What was that?" Butter asked.

Donald continued to kiss and suck on her neck. "That ain't nothing but the TV." Butter slowly began to relax again until Donald began taking off her lingerie.

"Baby, let's go to bed."

"Tamela, you're always the main person saying I ain't spontaneous. Let's stay right here."

As he continued kissing and not giving her space to leave the sofa, Butter gave in to the mood and allowed him to undress her. She felt awkward because the TV would continue to break her concentration. However, her worst fear was about to come true.

Now finally undressed, her husband eased on top of her, ready to penetrate and get the job over with so he could get back to his game.

"Don't force it. I'm dry and I'm cold, too. Why don't you grab a sheet or something from the room to keep me warm?"

"I can keep you warm...here, take this." Donald tossed his shirt to her. "Put that on."

"That's dirty! Don't put that on me. You had it on at work."

"It ain't going to take that long."

Butter looked at Donald with a *no you didn't say what I thought you said* look on her face. "What do you mean, 'It won't take that long?' I don't want a rush job. If you're not going to do it right then don't do it at -"

A sound other than the TV stopped Butter from finishing her statement. As the couple's attention focused on the source of the sound, their mouths dropped open.

"What?" asked Billy as he looked at his mother's naked body lay across the sofa and then looked at his stepfather's naked body.

"Billy!" *Oh my goodness* she thought to herself as she became red with embarrassment. "Billy, go to bed!"

"I just wanted to pee and to get some soda."

Donald quickly stood and, with a rock-hard dick, walked toward Billy. "You heard what your mother said, little nicca. Go to bed!"

If looks could kill, Donald would have died on the spot because Billy shot him a murderous look before slowly turning around and taking his time to go inside his room. "You ain't my father," Billy said, and as he entered his room, Donald grabbed the knob and slammed the door shut.

Donald was fuming with anger. Not only could he not finish his video game, and not only did a child embarrass him and his wife, but the little boy got smart with him and he couldn't take matters into his own hands and spank him like he wanted to because it was his stepson. "You lucky I ain't your father," he yelled at the door. From the other side of the door he could hear the voice of an eight-year-old say, "I wish you would hit me!" Donald tucked his lips under his teeth and placed his hand on the knob to go inside and show the little boy who was the man.

"Donald! What are you doing?" Butter had already dressed and now was rushing toward Donald.

"He's in there getting smart! He don't talk to me like that!" Donald yelled now pointing at the door.

"Let's go," Butter said while grabbing his massive arm and pulling him down the hall to their bedroom. As the door closed she began her verbal fury. "You don't call him a nicca or whatever! You didn't have to butt in at all because I already had told him what to do. He is a child. The way you ran over to him you would think he was a grown man. This is your home, not the club. You are not working security in here. And then you have the nerve to go over there and slam the door."

"He was getting smart!"

"That's beside the point! He's still a child. Going to call somebody a nicca – a child at that." Butter placed her glasses on and finally could focus on her target. "If you can't act like an adult then I'll discipline him, not you."

"You ain't disciplined him yet! He's still being smart and disrespectful. You know he doesn't like me."

"And you make it worse by feeding into it. Once again, Donald, he is a child. Of course he's going to resent his mother being with another man, but you don't make it easy on him. You yell at him...kicked him out of the bachelor suite before we got married...you never want to do anything with him...you always..."

Donald sat on the bed and listened to her long list of his wrongdoings with sarcasm in his eyes. He was sick of Butter and her mouth and he damn sure was sick of her son. "Billy ain't never treat that nicca Daren like that." As Butter sat in astonishment of Daren's name being brought up, Donald felt a reversal of power. "Yeah, that's what I thought."

"You ain't think shit! He never treated Daren like that because Daren was nice to him and played with him. When did you ever do that?"

Donald grew even angrier that his sudden gain in power disappeared. He felt like he had to go for the kill before he lost the entire argument. "I know you ain't about to look me in my face and give another nicca props over me! I know you ain't."

Butter sighed and lay under the sheets in silence trying to ignore Donald's words. She then began to cry at the hurt her heart was feeling. She had good intentions for the night and they suddenly went bad. To make matters worse, Donald continued to ridicule her.

"That's what I thought. Talking that Daren shit to me."

"You brought him up," Butter cried out.

"I don't give a fuck who brought him up! Fuck him! Where's that nicca at now? Huh? He wouldn't even marry you and you bring his ass up. Fuck him! Now say something. I dare you!"

CHAPTER 10

Butter returned from her lunch break feeling more relaxed than before her break. The stress from being embarrassed in front of her son was shaming her, and the friction between Donald and Billy was breaking her spirit. There was absolutely no peace in her own home and she was uncomfortable there. Donald still came in late from doing security at the club and he also continued to sleep on the sofa. It bothered her to get her son and his daughter up and ready for school in the morning by herself, and then they had to walk past Donald before they left. Sometimes Butter would try to wake him and tell him to go to bed before she woke the kids, but her efforts were useless because he wouldn't budge. Strangely enough, she began to enjoy going to work and answering phones because it was a break away from the drama.

Butter sipped the last bit of soda from her McDonald's cup and dropped it in the trash. She then focused her attention to the flashing light on her phone, which read that she had four messages. The first three were customers needing assistance. She jotted down their information and played the fourth message and suddenly the stress, that once faded from her being, rushed back and she felt a headache coming on.

"Hello, this is Ms. Parker, your son's teacher. We have been having a difficult time with him today. Please call me at (301) 773..." Without hesitation, Butter hung up and began dialing.

"Rose Elementary, this is Ms. Parker."

"Hello, this is Billy Walker's mother. What's going on?"

"Thank you for calling so promptly. Billy has been refusing to do any work. He won't participate in our lessons, he won't read, or talk. All that he does is draw pictures of himself and who I assume to be his family. This little problem began recently."

"Oh? He's drawing instead of doing his work? I'll take care of him when he gets home."

"It's more serious than that, Mrs. Walker."

"It's Smith. I just got married."

"Then that explains everything."

"That explains what?"

"In these pictures there are always five people; two men, a woman, and a little boy and girl. The little boy, who I assume to be Billy, is shooting the taller man."

A chill went down Butter's spine. The thought of Billy drawing pictures of death made a wave of panic go through her body. *Is Billy just being an angry child or is he contemplating murder? Does he hate Donald that much?* she thought to herself. *This absolutely can not be happening*. Butter began visualizing Billy pulling a trigger and killing Donald.

"Mrs. Smith?"

"The sound of Ms. Parker's voice snapped Butter back into reality. "Yes, where is Billy now? Put him on the phone, please."

"I'm sorry, but since we couldn't get in touch with you we notified his grandmother, Mrs. Bell. That's your mother, right?"

"That's correct."

"Okay. I wasn't sure because you, your mother, and your son all have three different last names. Anyway, your mother told us that she'd notify Billy's father and he came right over and picked him up."

Butter couldn't believe her ears. Now William wanted to all of a sudden be responsible and be a father? *Maybe he's finally maturing*, Butter thought, but she didn't like for Billy being around him too long because of his foul language and bad influence. As her mind drifted off, her phone clicked informing her of an incoming call.

"Thank you, Ms. Parker. I'll straighten

this matter out. Bye," and she switched to the second line. "Hello?"

"I ought to fuck you up," came a man's voice over a pounding rap music beat. It had to be William.

"Excuse me? What did you say?"

"You heard me. I ought to fuck you up. Got some motherfucka trying to bully my son and threatening him."

"Where's Billy?" Butter asked trying to gather her thoughts. "Is he okay?"

"He's fine now that he's with me. You need to concern yourself with your husband."

"William, you need to watch your mouth when you talk to me."

"I ain't gotta watch shit! How are y'all going to try to fuck in front of my son? What kind of mother are you? Going to let some dude just do whatever and think I wasn't gonna do shit about it? I'm a fuck him up!"

Butter tried to stay calm, but her heart began beating rapidly. "Stop discussing adult business around my son."

"My son needs to hear this. He needs to know that Daddy, his real daddy, has his back and will protect him. Tell your husband that I'm coming for him."

Butter's head felt like it was about to explode and her heart sped up even more. "William, don't go there. Please don't go there. We can sit down and talk this out."

"Why was y'all fuckin' in front of him?"

"It wasn't like that!"

"Then how was it then?"

"William, I'm at work. Let's talk about this later."

"I want to talk about it now 'cause I know my son ain't no liar. Tell me your side of the story."

"Why do you always got to start something?"

"Bitch, I ain't start shit! Your mother called me! You and your husband started this shit and I'm a finish it."

"I'll pick Billy up later."

"Bring your husband with you. And he better have a gun."

"Bye, William."

"I know where his punk-ass work, too."

"Bye," and with those words Butter slammed down the receiver. "Why me, Lord?" she said aloud unknowingly, and she placed both hands over her face and inhaled slowly trying to calm herself.

"Tamela," said Butter's coworker in the next cubicle. "The head honcho wants to see you."

Butter stood and walked to her boss' office. "Yes, you need to see me?"

"Tamela, please discontinue using the phones for your personal calls or find somewhere else to work. You've been back from your break over a half an hour and you haven't taken a call yet. I'm docking you those thirty minutes."

Butter spun around and left his office without saying another word. She ran straight through the call center to the restrooms and collapsed into tears. She flipped open her cellular phone and called Donald.

*   *   *

That damn Angela has been a thorn in my ass since day one. Finally I have her father up here to assist me in putting an end to this madness. It's hard to teach with her in the classroom.

"Mr. Brown?"

"Yes, sir. You're Mr. Stanley? Angela's father?"

"Yes."

This fool looks like he got dressed in the dark. He has on a checkered brown and beige sports coat, black slacks that expose his ankles, which are inside dark green socks, a navy blue shirt, gray cap, and some old penny loafers with pennies in them. Oh my goodness. Please, God, don't let me laugh in his face. Is that Brut that I smell? Forgive me, God, but I'm about to laugh. Please update this man's wardrobe to the new millennium or send the fashion police to whip his ass.

"Mr. Brown, are you okay? What's so funny?"

"Oh, nothing. I'm just having a good day. I love that cologne. What is it?"

"It's Brut, man. It's a classic."

A classic? You's a damn fool! I wore

Brut back in seventh grade, and the women slapped me for wearing it. And you got the nerve to still have it on? "Yes, it is a classic. I have some at home." But I ain't worn that funk since I attended Benjamin Tasker Middle School. "Here's your daughter." Angela was escorted by the secretary who waved and closed the door after Angela entered.

"Why they bring me up here? I'm missing recess and all of the fun."

"I don't want to hear it, Angela. Didn't I tell you to do your work and stop acting up?"

"Yes," Angela replied with a very angelic, sweet voice. Her eyes were focused on the floor.

"Then why is Mr. Brown telling me you're acting up? Why should I give you money when you ask for it? Why should I buy you that bike you want? Do you still want that bike?"

As Mr. Stanley continued grilling Angela, I felt as happy as those large sistahs in the front row of the strip clubs. I have never seen Angela bow down to anybody. Look at her looking all innocent and confused. I got her ass this time. She didn't think I would find her father's contact information. I finally have my class back in my power.

Recess ended and my class arrived at my door. Mr. Stanley and I shook hands and he left after one more statement, "Angela, don't forget what I said. No bike for you if you don't straighten up your act," and he walked away. The class is normally a little rowdy after recess, but never this much. They are bouncing off of the walls and off of each other. Something's wrong. "Alanah, what's going on?"

"Mr. Brown, the class is in an uproar because James did the Stone Cold Stunner on Winston. They were fighting and James was pretty angry."

I knew that Alanah would tell me exactly what happened. She is the brightest, smartest, and the sweetest student. If I have a daughter I'll name her Alanah. "James, Winston, in the hall," and as I separate the source of the action, everyone settles down and begins the afternoon warm-up. I then quietly creep into the hall to see James pouting. I really like James because he is into sports, the girls like him, and he hits the books hard; reminds me of myself when I was his age – just cool for no reason. "What happened, James?"

"I was playing wrestling with Rico and 'em and Winston was playing Double-Dutch with the girls. He kept coming over there and touching my leg. I don't know why he kept messing with us. He should have just stayed over there and jumped rope."

Now James was cool, but Winston was another story. He was sweeter than Alanah, but that isn't cool when you're a boy. He loved jumping rope and had the nerve to have Lil' Bow Wow pictures on his notebook with little red hearts that he drew on the pictures that read "WT loves LBW" – Winston Taylor loves Lil' Bow Wow. Sometimes when another student brought up Lil' Bow Wow or sang one of his songs, Winston would say, "Girl, he is so fine." I told James to go back into the class, and I gave a short lecture to Winston on what behavior is appropriate and inappropriate. Never had to explain what those words meant to him because he knew everything. When I reentered the class with Winston, I find Angela standing at another student's desk with her fist cocked back.

"Say something else! I dare you! That's why your mother don't love you now, because you don't know how to act. Say something and watch me steal you in your mouth." Angela then began to jump at the other student.

I call Angela into the hallway. "Angela, your father just left here five minutes ago. Have you forgotten what he told you? He may be in the parking lot. Do I need to call him back up here?"

"Please, I don't know that man."

"What do you mean 'you don't know that man'? He's your father, ain't he?"

"He supposed to be, but I only seen him about three or four times."

"This year?"

"In my life."

"Does he call you?"

"No. My mother calls him sometimes and I've talked to him about once or twice in the past two years. He always talking about a bike, but I ain't seen one yet and it's been four years. I asked him for it in first grade and both times I was in second grade. I asked for it the first time in kindergarten; that was the first time I remember seeing him. He gave me two dollars that day talkin' 'bout that's my allowance. He gave my mother 50 dollars another time for me to get some school clothes and that's it! He aint' never going to give me no allowance, and when he does decide to get me a bike I'll be old enough to drive a car. He ain't my father."

My heart is hurting for Angela. I can feel her pain and it saddens me. Here I am shaking his hand and he is part of the reason that Angela is a tyrant in my class. However, this situation may be the solution to my problem.

*   *   *

"Tell William to bring it! He bad and shit, tell that motherfucka to bring it!" Donald was yelling with pure rage into the phone. "You crying for him?"

"No," said Butter. "I'm just sick of the drama and no one's going to hurt anybody. We are adults and there are children involved."

"Well, it's on him. This shit can go down any way he wants it to. I'll make your son a bastard."

"Why are you so ignorant?"

"Who you talkin' to? You takin' up for him like you did Daren that night?"

"I'm not taking up for anyone including you since you called my son a bastard."

"I ain't call him a bastard. I said I can make him a bastard. That means I'll kill his father and – "

Butter hung up the phone and dialed Robin. Before the phone began ringing she heard Robin's voice.

"What in the hell is going on? They calling upstairs talking saying, 'Robin, come get your friend.' They are acting like you're having a nervous breakdown or something. Girl, take this tissue and blow your nose." Robin handed Butter a wad of toilet paper. "Now what's going on? Is it Donald again?"

"Yes and no," Butter's voice was muffled by the tissue as she began blowing.

"Tamela, we have about three hours left to work. Come over here and wash your face, get yourself together, and get back to your job. We'll discuss this after work at Club Dream or somewhere, but you can't be bringing that personal stuff to work. Handle that shit outside of these walls. Don't let them see you broken down like this."

"I know, but it was so much stuff happening."

"I care, but they don't and they will fire your ass. Your personal business is to be handled behind closed doors. Now go out there with your mask on and act like nothing has happened. We have three hours left. Just hold on, and at five o'clock, you can let it all out. Until then, swallow the stress and drama. Don't have them people around your cubicle call me again!"

***

As my students and I returned to the classroom from recess, I notice Winston and his mother waiting at the door.

"Mr. Brown, I want to talk to James! He has no business hitting my son. I had to take him to the doctor this morning."

"Hold on," I say and I calmly usher my kids into the room and get them started on their work. "Okay," I say to Winston's mother, "I won't allow you to talk to James without his mother being here, but I will allow you to listen to his side of the story." I then bring James out. "James, tell us what happened yesterday."

"Well," James begins as he looks down to the floor, "all of the boys were playing wrestling and Winston was playing jump rope with the girls. He then came over and touched my privates."

"What?!" I yell in astonishment. I can't believe what I just heard.

Winston's mother looked shocked and she put her arm around her son. "That's okay, Mr. Brown. I'll take care of everything."

"You have to get your son some counseling! He can't be harassing my students."

"I will, Mr. Brown. I'm sorry about this."

Winston never said a word.

CHAPTER 11

I've been doin' the damn thing with Marcy. Last night she and I strolled through Georgetown holding hands, talking, and carrying on like lovers do. Ain't made love to her yet, but we've been making lovely conversation. Last night, although the streets were packed, I pulled her into my warm embrace and gave her a long, seductive, juicy kiss. I just spontaneously slipped my tongue into her mouth in the middle of our conversation, and the busy sidewalk of people had to walk around us while gazing at the site of pure passion.

As we pulled away she looked into my eyes and said, "I need stuff like that in my life. You are good for the soul. I feel like I'm 16 whenever I'm around you." Thoughts of being in her presence make driving home from work in this terrible DC traffic a little easier. There goes my cell phone.

"Hello?"

"Guess what I'm doing?

"Marcy, I was just thinking about us kissing in front of them people last night. We had a good time, didn't we?"

"Guess what I'm doing, Daren?"

"What?"

"I'm tasting myself," Marcy says seductively.

"Is that right? How does it taste?"

"It tastes real good, sort of like candy, but if you want to know what flavor then you have to try it yourself. My pussy tastes better than my kiss."

"If it tastes that good then I have to taste it. Save me some."

"I sure will. Where are you?" Marcy asks, still using her seductive voice.

"I'm on 295 slowly getting closer to South Capitol. The traffic is terrible."

"Good. Take Suitland Parkway to avoid the traffic congestion and then get on Pennsylvania and come out here. I want to feed you this delicious pussy while we make a movie."

"A movie?"

"I got a few fantasies to share with you. Just hurry up and get here. Call me when you get near Upper Marlboro."

***

Butter hesitated to answer the phone after looking at the Caller I.D. She took a deep breath and picked up the receiver. Her heart began beating faster and faster, but she tried her best to speak calmly.

"Good afternoon. This is Tamela Smith at NIH."

"Tamela, does William drive an old, brown Cadillac?"

"Yes, why? Leave him alone."

"There you go being on his side!"

"I just don't want no trouble. That's my son's father and -"

"I don't need you to tell me that! How many times are you going to throw that in my face? Huh? I know I'm not your son's father!" After hearing no response he continued. "I asked because that fool has been parked outside of our apartment. I'm looking at him now."

"He has Billy. Maybe he's dropping him off."

"That ain't what he's doing. He's been out there for 20 minutes. I don't see Billy in the car, either."

"Well, don't go out there."

"This is my home. I'm not going to hide in here because of him. Thug life, baby! I'm a soldier...I'm a soldier! I'm a go out there and put the 9 Millimeter to his head."

Butter began to panic. "A gun? You have a gun in our home with our kids?"

"No, but I'll get one. I can call Mark right now and he'll bring it over here."

He sounds like a sucker, talking about

his friend's gun, Butter said to herself and began to chuckle. Suddenly the stress disappeared. *He's scared. All that talk and no action.*

***

Pulling into Marcy's driveway, I stare in awe of her home's splendor and its beauty. As soon as Marcy opens the door I greet her with a big hug and a passionate kiss. She smiles and leads me upstairs to her bedroom. Upon entering I can't help but to admire her king-size bed. Everything from the bedroom set to the art on the walls is top quality. I can tell they are expensive. And the room smells so good. Mmmm, being in here makes me want to come. I understand why she was touching and tasting herself.

"Daren, baby, get comfortable," Marcy says from her walk-in closet.

I begin kicking off my shoes and almost trip on something. What the...? This woman has a bear skin rug and I nearly tripped on the head. Damn, this is nice! And the bedroom window is so tall and wide and it has a nice view overlooking a golf course. Sitting down I discover that she has a waterbed. I light her huge candles, close the blinds, and I get undressed to my silk boxers. The only reason that I have them on is because all of my other drawers are dirty.

"You okay in there, Daren?"

"Yes. What are you doing?" I want her fine ass in here with me.

"I'm trying to find my outfit for scene one."

Tired of waiting, I go into the closet and find her bent over going through some bags. All she has on is the Teddy that she answered the door in and her caramel ass is peeking from under it. I can't help but to quietly get on my knees and kiss her left hip.

"Daren...oooh, you scared me. I'm not used to company, let alone in my closet."

My response is licking her inner thigh, and as the sound of her going through the bags ceases, I try to stretch my tongue between her thighs to taste her pussy. On my hands and knees, while she's still bent over, I try hard to twist my neck between her legs. As my neck begins to cramp I lay on my back and slowly guide her down until she's comfortably sitting on my face. Since we have all evening I begin a smooth, generous, patient stroke with my tongue, not teasing, but rather entering the vagina slowly. I then feel both of her hands on my head as she gives off a long moan of satisfaction. Damn, I haven't even touched her clit or pulled my dick out of my silks, and she's close to being pleased already.

***

Butter convinced Donald to leave through the back exit of the apartment since William remained parked out front. Robin had suggested they get a restraining order, so she and her husband were on their way to the police station. During the course of the ten minute ride Donald kept saying, "I'm a kill that motherfucker. He don't know I'm a thug," over and over again. Butter struggled to keep a straight face as she thought to herself, *Yeah, right. You ain't hardly going to do nothing and you ain't no thug*. His silliness had her feeling a little better.

After signing all of the paperwork for the restraining order, Butter and Donald drove to William's mother's house and, as Butter suspected, Billy was there. Donald waited in the car while Butter assured William's mother that everything was okay. She thanked her for watching Billy and she took him back home with her and Donald.

***

"Daren, I could tell by how good you kissed that you could eat pussy good," Marcy said. She lay on her side with her arm holding her head up and she looked me in my eyes.

"You liked that? Did I do you right, baby?"

"Did you do it right? I came three or four times! And I came just the way I wanted to."

"And how is that?"

"In your face," and with that statement she starts to laugh. "Now we've been in here talking for over an hour. I can't believe this. You ate me out in my closet and then we stay here for another hour just talking. This is special. You're a special man. You make me do things that I've never done. Speaking of things I've never done, let's get this role playing started. Scene one begins downstairs in my living room."

Once situated on the plush leather sofa, Marcy comes from the kitchen with a bottle of Cristal and pours two glasses. I ain't never tasted that before. I can't even afford Dom. I then notice tears swelling in Marcy's eyes.

"Daren, this is a special night. I won't live to see tomorrow. I am terminally ill and I won't be around to enjoy the rest of your life. In my last day on earth there's no one I'd rather be with than my man, and no place I'd rather be than in his arms. And since you are my man...I need you. Please, hold me. Look me in my eyes and reassure me of how special I've been to your life." The tears begin to stream down her cheeks and her voice begins to tremble. "I'm going to miss you, Daren, so please cherish our last moment together. Hold me, Daren. Kiss me and make love to me for the last time. But first, tell me how you feel about me."

A lump swells in my throat as I take a second sip of Cristal. This stuff tastes good. "Marcy, our past is one that others dream to experience in their future. We've traveled to beautiful places, enjoyed extravagant events, and relished in each other's presence. You've made my life complete and I owe all of the happiness of my days and the passion of my nights to you. Falling asleep holding you and waking up to your beautiful eyes are the small things that mean so much. I can only imagine how hard life will be without you. We've made sensuous love. We've felt the other's soul. Every kiss of your lips is like a dream come true – a fantasy being sensually achieved. We love spontaneously and with so much emotion that no other love will ever surpass what we have combined to become. So, while you're here, let's take advantage of what time we have left and polish what stands to be the greatest love the world has ever witnessed."

Marcy reveals an emotional smile as her tears are smeared by her hands as new tears begin to form and flow. "That was beautiful and so romantic. Where did you get those words? I need to go get some tissue."

Before she can turn to go upstairs I pull her close to me and give her another kiss and a tight hug. *Marcy, there was a woman that I think I used to love and I said to you what I always wanted to say to her. However, something felt a little too right about expressing those sentiments.*

"I'll be right back," Marcy says after I release my hug. As she walks upstairs I follow her from a distance. Once I hear water running I grab the comforter from the foot of the bed, grab her candles, her hand-held mirror from her vanity, and I run downstairs. On the living room floor I set up a romantic palate with a vase of roses and our Cristal by candlelight. Once she returns her mouth drops open and her lingerie slowly falls. I undress and proceed to seductively kiss her body from her neck to her calves and then to her toes. I then hold the mirror next to my face and begin slowly licking her lower lips. She giggles and adjusts the mirror so that she can better see the action between her legs. As I begin to really lick, tongue, and tease, her giggling stops and the moaning begins. After making her come again we tenderly make love.

***

"Would you stop saying that, Donald?" Butter asks as she cuts her eyes at him.

"I'm a thug. Fuck him! Let him keep showing off and I'm a flex on him."

"You talking about my daddy?" Billy asks while looking over his Happy Meal.

"Stay out of grown folk's business, little boy," Donald replies.

"Stop discussing grown folk's business in front of him then," Butter answers."

"I pay the rent up in here!"

"And it's barely more than the note of your truck!" Butter shot back.

"And your point is?"

"My point is that I can pay the rent. If it will make you talk like you have some sense around here, then I'll pay the rent and you pay for that truck you went and got without my knowledge. I can't believe you're driving around *in my honeymoon*."

"Tamela, stop talking about this in front of your son!" Donald yells with an embarrassed look of disgust.

"Aw stop crying, Donald," Butter said softly as she placed some French fries into her mouth.

Donald then grabbed the car keys and stood.

"Where are you going?"

"I'm going into work early," Donald snarled.

"Two hours early?"

"Yup." With those words Donald slammed the door.

***

"Daren, isn't this beautiful?" Marcy asks while staring at the sunset.

"Yes, baby, it's lovely." I then kiss her forehead and she closes her eyes and smiles.

"You know, Daren, how you spoke to me in the living room, how you held me, kissed me, looked into my eyes, and made love to me?"

"Um-hmm..."

"That's how it should always be. It should always be special and sentimental, not just for me, but for all women. Love should not hurt; it should be kind, gentle, patient, and sweet, and you seem to understand that.

Whoever ends up with you will have something special. You are ahead of your time...far beyond your years. I see why you have a hard time finding women your age."

I twist myself further and plant a soft kiss on her lips.

"Daren, I know that I can't have you because you want kids and you want to do the family thing. However, I'm going to take advantage of my time with you. If only you were older...if only you were older."

***

Donald grew impatient due to his frustration from the situation with William watching the apartment and the rest of the drama. "If it wasn't for the fact that he is my wife's son's father I would have put the 9 Millimeter to him a long time ago. I would feel bad if I had to live with my stepson after killing his father. So can you help me? I don't want him dead, I just want him out of the picture."

Officer Anthony Wright looked Donald in the eyes without revealing how little respect he had for him. A stepson would not have stopped Anthony. He was about 6'3" and had an average build, not skinny, but not muscular either. He would have buried anyone watching his house and stalking his family – no questions asked. The loud music in the club made it easier for him to think.

He thought to himself about how his reason for doing security was different than all of the bouncers' reasons. They did security full-time to put food in their kids' mouths and a roof over their heads. Anthony worked as a policeman full-time and did security just to keep his ear to the street. He could learn more about what was happening just by hanging around in the club a few hours a week.

"You want your wife's baby's father out of the picture? What, make him leave town or put him in jail?"

"Arrest him! If you -"

"Who the fuck are you raising your voice at?"

"I'm sorry. I just got excited," Donald said calmly as he looked into Officer Anthony's merciless eyes. "If you make him leave town he'll just come back."

"Alright, Donald. I'll take care of him. A favor for a favor, understand? I'll take care of this guy with no problem. Just make sure you jump when I need you to collect some information on this guy because I can't keep up with him."

"You need me to watch somebody? Who?"

"His name is Daren Brown."

CHAPTER 12

Donald was enthused about the name that Officer Wright said to him. He walked out of the office where they had just talked with the name "Daren Brown" dancing in his head. He knew that it had to be his nemesis; the man that his wife loved before him and wanted to marry, the man that gave her the nickname "Butter" that she still couldn't get rid of, the man that he beat-out for his wife, but still felt like he was inferior to.

Since day one he lived in Daren's shadow because Robin always described him as being so "perfect" for Tamela, and she never disagreed. Sometimes he even thought that he noticed a smile appear across her face, which made him even more upset. He knew that Robin didn't care too much for him marrying Tamela because if she did she wouldn't make little gestures and say snide remarks about him. Just her bringing up Daren's name in Donald's presence made him feel disrespected. He knew Robin didn't like him and he didn't like her either.

Now was his chance to build himself up by putting Daren down. All that he had to do was find a little extra information about Daren that could make him not look so great in Tamela's eyes. Donald had no idea what he was looking for, but he would be able to recognize it if it came across his path. He stood at the front door of the club with his head in a fog from the thought of Daren and how much he had actually grown to hate him.

And then there was the matter with William. Donald wasn't scared, but he had no idea what William would try to do. Although he wanted to beat Billy, he hadn't, so there was no reason for William to be upset with him. He felt that if he cared so much then he would get custody and not have to worry about him being in any harm. Plus, Billy must have lied to his father and made up a story. Whatever the case, Donald didn't feel like he did any wrong in the situation. It bothered him that he had a child in his home that he couldn't discipline. It made him feel like he was king over the entire home until it came to Billy; that part of the "kingdom" was ruled by Butter, but Donald wanted total control. However, having Billy get away with making certain statements and getting smart with him made him feel like less of a man because he couldn't do anything about it directly. He would always have to run to Butter so that she could handle it.

Donald hoped that Officer Wright could handle William because he feared the unknown. At the same time, Donald was upset about Officer Wright yelling at him minutes ago. He was glad that there was no one around to see it because he would have been embarrassed. At the same time he knew that he wouldn't have said anything if someone was around to see it. He feared Officer Wright. Not only was he a real policeman, but he had witnessed the wrath of violence that he had brought to some people. That's the main reason that he went to him with the William situation.

"Hi, Sam," said a sweet masculine voice.

Donald snapped out of his deep thoughts only to find a man standing in front of him with a group of women. The man stood about 5'7" and he wore earrings, much eyeliner, lipstick, and a foundation on his mocha skin. His hair was short and his frame was pretty thin. He couldn't have been more than 160 pounds. Nestled in with his crew of beautiful females, it was hard to tell that he wasn't one when they stayed together. But when alone, it was clear that this was a man passing as a woman.

The man stood with three women as they waited for their other two friends to stop chatting with the other bouncer and come through the door. While waiting, the man smiled at Donald, whispered something to the women that he was with, and they all turned around and looked at Donald. They then began to chuckle.

Donald put a mean look on his face.

"Oh," said the man, "so now you can't speak to nobody, Sammy?"

All of the attention in the lobby area quickly focused on Donald. Not only was the man and his female crew smiling at him, but so was a group of other clubbers that were hanging around, and so was the other bouncer.

Donald walked over to the man that kept saying hi and threw a solid punch at him, which struck him in his left eye. The man hit the ground instantly and was out cold, but his eyes remained open. The lobby area was in shock, but Donald kept going. He grabbed the man by his head and neck and lifted him up.

The crew of women, which now numbered five, were yelling, "Leave Trey alone! Get off of him!" A few of them even pulled on Trey to rescue him while the others began hitting Donald. It didn't matter, Donald threw Trey out of the door onto the hard concrete.

"One of y'all bitches hit me again and I'm a stretch one of y'all out just like I did your little gay friend."

"You didn't have to hit him like that! He always comes to this club!" one of Trey's friends screamed at Donald.

Donald turned his back to the woman. "Since he comes here a lot he should have known not to fuck with me. If you really care about your little gay friend then you'd call him an ambulance." Donald walked back into the lobby area and stood next to the other bouncer who was laughing at the spectacle.

"You knocked him slam the fuck out! Good punch," and with those words he gave Donald some dap. He had no clue that Donald wouldn't be embarrassed if he could help it. It was bad enough that Officer Wright had just yelled at him and made him feel less than a man. He had to do something to get his machismo back.

CHAPTER 13

Anthony sat in an unmarked police car waiting for the group of teenagers to depart the area. If anything was about to happen he didn't want any witnesses. He listened to Dr. Dre's *Chronic 2001* album, which played low enough to only barely break the silence. Nevertheless, the music could not break his thoughts of Marcy and how their relationship ended. His mind flashed the arguing and the deceit that came out of nowhere. He understood why Marcy left him, after all, a woman can't put up with her husband's cheating but for so long. He just wished that he hadn't been so blatant to cheat in her face.

That's in the past, he thought. But what is in the present is the fact that he stood to lose all of the assets that he and Marcy bought during all of those years. All that he got was his car, stereo, big-screen TV, and a huge wardrobe of the finest clothes that a man could wear. On the other hand, Marcy got the house and everything else. She even bought a condo and allowed her mother to live in the house while Anthony lived in a house of lesser quality. He felt that despite his actions, he should have received more. Out of the five cars, a house, and all of the stocks and mutual funds, all that he got was a car and some material items. He took them because at the time they were what he used, but looking back he realized that he lost. That became evident when he saw Marcy driving a sparkling new Jaguar shortly after their separation and agreement.

The agreement was abrupt and Anthony only conceded once Marcy had him by the balls. The day that Marcy got tired of dealing with the lies and chose to stand up to him showed him that he had lost all control over her. In an attempt to scare her into seeing things his way he pulled out his gun, cocked it, and placed it above her left ear. The urine streaming down her leg was evident of her being scared, but her eyes didn't give in and she refused to see things his way. She was tired of him bullying her and she wouldn't ever agree with him again. He realized that it was over and that he needed to leave before he got in trouble for murdering her. Without thinking over his words he told her to keep whatever he didn't take and that he would only come back to sign the divorce papers.

He now felt that if he played his cards right he could get half of the house, half of the condo, a couple of cars, half of the investments, and maybe even her new Jaguar. He would definitely show Marcy how precise he could be and how much power he had. She would surely feel his wrath by way of her diminished bank account.

The sight of two boys leaving the group of teenagers broke Anthony's thoughts. He began to grow optimistic that the scene would be clear soon, but then he saw his "pigeon" walk out from the side of the apartment building where the remaining teens stood. Anthony disregarded them and focused on his prey. He didn't care if there were witnesses at that point. He turned the light switch to off so that once his door opened, the light on the ceiling wouldn't come on and draw any attention to him. He slowly cracked the door, eased out while stooping down, and made his way to the man that was walking to the brown Cadillac. Anthony pulled the gun out of his jacket and cocked it. The man unlocked his car door and sat down, but before he could close it, Anthony was up on him with the gun out.

"William, don't move, motherfucka, or I'll blow your ass away."

William became relaxed. He knew that he would live to see the next day because if this person wanted him dead he would have pulled the trigger without saying a word. The only sound would have been that gun blasting into his flesh. William was relieved.

"Put your hands on the wheel and leave them there." William slowly turned toward the barrel of the gun as Anthony called for back-up and then patted his jacket. "Damn, William, you could've blasted me if you weren't sleeping," he said as he removed a .22 caliber gun from William's jacket. "Then again, this tiny weapon wouldn't hurt nobody. Stop being a cheap motherfucka and buy a real gun, punk. What the fuck you going to do with this baby gun? Be a man wit' yo shit." Anthony then reaches over and pulls a capsule from the cup holder. "Crack? William, you sell this shit or use it?"

"That ain't mine."

"Do you have some weed?"

"Look, that crack ain't mine and I don't have no weed."

"Either way you're going to jail. Say goodbye to your baby's momma. You have the right to remain silent. Anything you say can and will be..."

William heard that speech before. As he was cuffed and forced to lean on the side of the car, he looked on as several squad cars arrived. He felt helpless and embarrassed when the tenants came out and others peered through their windows. *Damn*, he thought to himself, *where did this bullshit come from? I was about to take care of Donald and I'm all of a sudden on my way to jail.*

The phone ringing sent Butter running to the receiver. Upon answering, she walked it to her husband who was busy playing Madden 2K1 on the Playstation.

"What?!" he yelled at her. He then took the phone from her hand. "Hello?"

"Don, I took care of that thing. That bird is cooped up in a cage."

"For real?" Donald asked without holding back his excitement. He jumped up from the sofa and the game controller fell to the floor. He then walked away from Butter and lowered his voice. "Did you beat him up for me? Did you plant the drugs in his car like you said you were?" Less than a minute later he hung up the phone and continued playing the game with a huge smile on his face.

"Good news?" Butter asked. "Care to share?"

Donald couldn't think of a lie quick enough to respond. "Baby, let's do it."

Butter's eyes damn-near popped out of their sockets. All that she heard was her husband using a term of "endearment" and using his word for sex. Not taking any chances on hesitating, she grabbed his hand, pulled him to the bedroom, and got undressed. It had been months since the last time they made love and it was wonderful. Not only did Donald go down on her, but he actually tongue kissed her. It had been a long time since he did that. She didn't know what that phone call was about, but she hoped that more of them would come in the future.

CHAPTER 14

A lot has changed in the past couple of months. For starters, I called Country last month and...

"Hey, baby. What are you up to tonight? I have a steaming, hot, delicious, *Meat Supreme* pizza for you. Would you like it delivered tonight?"

"I can't order anymore, Daren," she said in a voice that seemed insecure.

"Country, you got your steak?" I asked anxiously.

"Yes, and he doesn't know that you exist. He thinks I've been a *virgin* since my divorce."

And so did I. You told me the same thing. You could have easily been sexing someone after your divorce but before me. You're cool, but sneaky. I actually believed that shit you said, but I respect your game.

"Daren, are you there?"

"I'm here."

"Well, you're pizza is supreme and it's the best that I've ever had, but I don't want to spoil what I have going on with my steak, if you know what I mean."

"I understand. Enjoy yourself."

"Thank you for understanding. Bye, Daren."

She's been out of my life ever since, but when one door closes another opens. I've actually had two doors open for me. The first was this fine woman that's from North Philly named Naya. She's a student at Howard University. We've been kicking it hard. I pick her up late at night and take her motorcycle riding. Sometimes we ride at 1 and 2:00 in the morning to Powder Mill Road because deer come onto the back roads around that time. She and I watch them and afterwards we go back to her place and make love. Whenever Howard University had her stressed I would come over and help her relieve it. She is such a passionate and tender lover - lil' young thang. She is beautiful with the sweetest, dark skin, bright smile, pretty eyes, and angelic voice.

The other open door is Raquel, the woman that was my sixth grade sweetheart; the one that I met at Zanzibar after my rough, first week of school. Well, she is no longer married and she did a search on the internet and found me. She and I have been kicking it very hard – hitting the movies, candlelight dinners, playing cards, Scrabble, and doing whatever we feel.

When we aren't in bed making love, we're busy laughing and enjoying the other's company. Raquel is a church girl. She actually sings in the choir. I normally go to New Temple when I do attend church, but that hasn't stopped Raquel from begging me to come to her church. I told her that I'll be out to see her sing. I have to support my baby.

If Raquel continues to be so compatible, then I'll definitely get her a diamond ring and propose. For now I'm going to continue hooking up with Marcy and Naya every now and then. I still even have Aunt Mike available, but Country was the bomb. I wish that she was still here.

CHAPTER 15

Officer Anthony Wright smiled at the precise details that were being told to him.

"So that's the girl from Howard, the one from Bowie named Raquel, and your wife Marcy," Donald signified while handing two sheets of paper to Anthony. "Here are their addresses and an account of Daren's visits with each of them.

Anthony continued to smile in amazement while glancing over the papers. "This is pretty good," he said as he began reading more precise information that Donald didn't mention. "I know that Daren is the only man that my wife has been seeing."

"Yup."

"But he's been cutting my wife back and spending more time with this Raquel?"

"Yup. He used to stop in about two or three times a week over your wife's and would spend the night there sometimes. Now it's like he lives with Raquel and her daughter. He's always there and he ain't even been over your wife's recently." Donald stares at Anthony in total confusion of his motives.

Anthony unknowingly begins to scratch his chin in deep thought and begins to talk aloud forgetting that he isn't alone. "That's not good...that's not good. Raquel is not part of my plan."

"What plan?" There is only silence after Donald broke Anthony's concentration with his last question. "And I don't understand why you want him to be with your wife."

Anthony started to shoot verbal darts at Donald and tell him some things that he didn't understand about him either, but he had bigger fish to fry. "Some things aren't meant to be known and understood by everyone." Anthony didn't bother to acknowledge Donald's presence any further. He just folded the papers and walked away.

"So, you're Daren? How are you?"

I don't know who this man is. I hope he ain't trying to pick me up or nothing. How does he know my name? I'm going to stop coming to Friday's in Greenbelt, especially on Fridays because it's crowded as I don't know what in here.

"Am I supposed to know you?"

"No, but you know my wife Marcy." Anthony, with a nonchalant expression, continued, "Look, you're a man and I am, too. I'm going to be straight with you, I need you to cut back on Raquel and spend more time with my wife."

"What's up? I mean what's the deal with that? I thought she was divorced. She's your wife?"

"Look, we're in the process of getting a divorce, and she's set to get all of our assets when it's final. I need to establish proof that she's been messing around so I can get what I deserve in the divorce settlement."

"Like what?"

"Like some shit you don't need to be concerned with. All you need to know is that I have a substantial amount of money to pay you if you'll just spend more time with Marcy. Just a few more months and everything will be over. I'll have some property, I'll have my divorce, and you'll get paid."

I can't do that to Marcy. She is cool peoples. Plus, I don't trust this man. My father told me to never get involved in other people's domestic disputes anyway.

"What's your name?"

"Officer Anthony Wright. Just call me Anthony. Now how much do I need to pay you?"

"I can't be bought."

"Bullshit. Everybody has a price."

"I ain't feelin' you, dawg. For real. That's y'all's business."

"Well, it became your business when

you started fucking her," Officer Wright said with authority as he sternly stared into Daren's eyes. He was not in the mood for any games. "Now how much do you need? You're a teacher and they don't make no money."

You're right about that shit! "And?"

"And everybody has a price."

"Not me."

"Five thousand dollars?"

"No."

"Eight thousand dollars?"

"No."

"Okay, ten thousand?"

Shit, now you're talking. I can do a lot with ten grand. "I ain't fuckin' with y'all's business. Ten thousand sounds good, but I can't do Marcy like that."

"That bitch got you trained like a fuckin' puppy. All you probably do is eat her pussy all day and night. She likes that shit. And she spoils you, too. Don't she? I know she does. She spoiled and whipped your young ass."

I ain't saying a word. If I was whipped I'd be there more often and we wouldn't be having this conversation. I'm just picking up as many details about Officer Wright as I can.

"I'll tell you what, Marcy's Pet, my final offer is 12 thousand. At least tell me you'll think about it."

As the server returns with my barbeque ribs I can finally enjoy what I came here for. "Okay, I'll think about it."

"Twelve thousand, Daren. I'll be in touch. Make sure that you spend more time with my wife. Just cut back a little on Raquel. And don't tell Marcy that we met because if you do, then I'll have to pay your Howard honey and Raquel a visit. I know you wouldn't want that. You can keep them, just spend more time with Marcy."

***

Raquel is looking good and my girl can sing, too. She just performed a solo of Yolanda Adams' "Open My Heart." She tore it up! I know I'm not Jesus, but it felt like she was singing to me. Although she's sitting with the choir and I'm sitting in the congregation watching her daughter, we're still flirting with each other with our eyes and our expressions. Well, it at least looked like she was flirting back when she was singing. Now who is that tapping me on my shoulder?

"Hi, Daren."

"Marcy? What's up, lady?" Damn, she's looking good.

"Welcome to my church," she says smiling. She then pulls out two pens and a pad, and she hands me a pen and begins writing:

Where have you been hiding
I ain't been hiding
Are you serious about someone yet
Yes, I'm here with her
Call me if it doesn't work out

After writing that she takes her pens and pad and puts them back into her purse.

I look up and see Raquel looking at me with piercing eyes. This must be how she looks when she gets upset because the woman looks like someone just stole something from her. Damn! I ain't even do nothing!

We're back at Raquel's apartment and things have been pretty smooth. I can tell that something is bothering her because she's been quiet since the ride home from church.

"Daren," Raquel calls from the kitchen. "Come here for a second, please."

I walk in and she's at the stove stirring something in a pot. She hits the wooden spoon on the rim of the pot a few times and then places it on the counter.

"What did that woman say to you in church?"

"She asked me where I've been."

"Is that right?" She raises her eyebrow as she looks through me. "You used to mess with Marcy?"

Here we go! Why does the world have to be so damn small? "I used to mess with her."

"How long ago?" She's still not blinking.

"I cut her back when you and I started getting serious."

"Oh, so I'm your rebound?"

"I didn't say that."

"You ain't said shit, Daren!"

"Look, calm down. She and I were messing around for a few months – nothing serious at all. I found someone that I truly care about so I'm finished with the games."

"And who might that be?" she says trying to be stern. "It can't be me. I'm singing songs, and happy to finally have you there in church with me, and you're sitting with another woman...in front of my daughter at that!"

"Raquel, don't hardly go there. No hugs, no kisses, not even a handshake. Don't make it bigger than it is. You saw everything that happened. It's all about you now. The future is you. I even told her that I was there with you."

"What did she say to make you tell her that?"

"She asked if I was seeing someone on the serious side, and I said 'I'm here with her.'"

"Did you say my name?"

Here we go! I was doing good in this discussion until she brought that up. It seems the more I talk, the worse things become. "No, I didn't say your name 'cause I didn't think she knew you."

"Uh-huh, you don't know who I know. You ain't tell her my name, but I'm supposed to believe I'm the woman of your future. It's all about me, huh? I'm supposed to believe that?"

"It's the truth. How do you know her anyway?"

"Don't worry about how I know her! She's a member of my church and she used to be in the choir with me. That bitch can't sing either. She was always fuckin' up our songs. That's why her ass ain't singing with us now."

"Dag, she's so bad that she got kicked out of the choir? That's messed up. I ain't never heard of that."

"That's probably why you never wanted to come to church with me, because you knew she was a member there and you would be busted, right?"

"No, that ain't it. I had no idea that she went to your church. I didn't even know that she went to church at all. We really weren't that close."

"Is that right? Y'all really weren't that close, huh?"

"No, we weren't that close."

"Well, did you fuck her?"

Man oh man oh man...how in the hell did we get to this point? I really don't know, but I love Raquel and I truly care about her being secure in this relationship. I really want this love to last. I think I'm going to have to tell her everything.

"Okay, Raquel. Let me tell you. Marcy's ex-husband is a police officer and he's been trying to pay me to see his wife...." I now explain the entire scenario to her.

Raquel looks at me as if she can see through me. "Am I supposed to believe all of that bull shit?"

"It's the truth."

"Why didn't you tell me earlier?"

"I didn't want to scare you off. I thought I could handle it without it ever coming up."

Raquel looks at me with a cautious look. "Alright, Daren. Don't mess up. I've been through a lot of shit messing with some of these no good men out here, including my ex-husband. I'm just being careful. I bring you around my daughter so you know I care about you. I don't bring just anybody around her. Just promise me you won't see Marcy anymore."

"I'm not seeing her, sweetie."

"Promise me."

"I promise you."

***

"Close your mouths. Don't let me catch who's talking."

"Davina's the one talking, Mr. Brown."

"Thank you, Latisha, but I didn't ask you." Walking these kids through the hallways is a chore, especially right after recess. They bounce off the walls and off of each other and their mouths are steadily moving. I'm glad we're almost at the library so I can have a break from them for an hour.

"I hate that man!" Angela yells. "Ooh! I hate that man! He stinks!" She points towards Mr. Jackson's classroom. He was her teacher the previous year and most of the students and staff didn't care for him.

"Angela, you don't know what to say out of your mouth?" I say looking at her with a serious expression. "Be nice to Mr. Jackson."

"I'm serious, Mr. Brown. He smells like old people smell. You ever smelled an old person before? He smells like old wood and moth balls."

I'm trying hard not to laugh in front of this *grown,* little girl. If I open my mouth I'm going to laugh, so I simply nudge her into the library and close the door. I'll laugh when I get back to my classroom. She's been so good since I've given her more attention and responsibility. As I open the door I begin to chuckle a little and then I'm interrupted.

"Mr. Brown."

I know that voice. I really didn't expect to hear it at work. "Why are you here? You all up in my space now. That ain't cool at all."

"Have you considered my offer of $12,000?"

"Officer –"

"Just call me Anthony."

"Anthony, I ain't messing with you and Marcy. I don't care how much money you got. Find another man to pay for that job."

"That's too hard. Plus, you're already in there, but you're fucking things up being with Raquel. How are you going to mess with two bitches that go to the same church? You're fucking up my plans, Daren. Just cut back on

Raquel a little bit. That's all that I'm asking. This will be the easiest 12 thousand you've ever made. Twelve thousand to fuck a bitch and now you wanna act like a bitch."

"Fuck you! You're following me around like a bitch. You ain't got nothing better to do with your time?"

"You going to do it or not?"

"I ain't doing shit."

"Okay, Daren. I asked you nicely." He then opens his jacket and reveals the gun tucked in his waist. "I tried to work with you. It's your life."

"You threatening to kill me?"

"I wouldn't do that, but I'm going to make you wish you were dead. I'm going to make you die living."

"Whatever! Be up out of here, slim. Leave." He slowly walks out of my door.

I wait two minutes and then walk to the front to see what Anthony is driving – an unmarked, silver Chevy. I quickly write down the tag number.

Instead of going home I go straight to Raquel's house. On the drive over I kept my eyes glued on my rearview mirror to see if Anthony was following me. That fool is crazy and I just know some shit is going to go down soon. I don't know how I got myself into this one.

The first thing I see when I walk through the door is Raquel's daughter talking on the telephone while watching music videos.

"Well, good afternoon," I say loudly, but jovial.

"I gotta go," she says into the phone and hangs up. "Hi, Mr. Daren."

"Who?"

"I mean *Friend*. Hi, *Friend*," and she begins to smile.

"Where's my hug?" I open my arms as she shyly walks toward me and hugs me. "How was your day at school?"

"Uh...uh...it was fine."

"What did you learn?"

"Uh...uh..."

"And you're in here watching videos and talking on the phone? Go cut the TV off and get your books out, sweetie. I know you have homework."

It's now two hours later and Raquel is finally home. I greet her at the door with a hug and a kiss, but something ain't right.

"How are you doing, sweetie? How was your day?"

"It was fine."

"You sound like your daughter," I say laughing.

"Where is she? Next door?"

"Yes. She finished her homework, and she and I checked it together so afterwards, I said that she could go out."

"Well, my day was fine till I found this envelope on my windshield."

"What's in it?"

"Take a look," she says extending it toward me. I pull out a stack of five pictures of Marcy and me talking. I begin analyzing each one for minute details. I haven't even been with Marcy or Naya, the girl at Howard University.

"Do you care to explain?" she says slowly in a deep voice.

"Raquel, these pictures are -"

"I was just beginning to trust you. You're messing with everybody. Who's that other girl?"

"That's Naya, but that's in the past."

"Daren, take whatever you have here and get out. I don't like where this is going. I can't trust you –got pictures on my wind-shield, people keep calling here and hanging up! You just aren't worth it. Your ass gotta go!"

"Raquel -"

"Take your Marvin Gaye and your Rick James CDs. Take your DVDs and your -"

"Raquel, look at these pictures!"

"I did already!"

"Look at the ring on my right hand. Remember I let you wear it months back? You still have it on, which means that these pictures were taken before I let you wear my ring."

Raquel begins smiling very hard after my words sank through her big head. "I'm sorry, Daren."

"Naw, I don't wanna hear it," and I jok-ingly turn my back and walk into the kitchen.

She can't help but to laugh at my imitation of how she acts when she gets upset. I want to playfully make her feel bad for jumping to conclusions. "Those pictures are from that policeman. He's mad because I won't help him by seeing Marcy, so he's trying to break us up."

"Don't walk away from me. Where are you going? I said I'm sorry," she says as she follows me into the kitchen. "Daren, I'm sorry."

"Naw, a second ago you told me to pack my shit." I look into her eyes while I'm smiling. "You told me, Marvin Gaye, and Rick James to leave. What? You want Phyllis Hyman and Mary J. Blige to leave, too.?"

"No," Raquel pleads while laughing. Then she looks over to the stovetop and notices the meal I prepared. "Oooh! You cooked dinner for us, too. I'm sorry, Daren. Mommy's sorry."

"Uh-huh! I'm in here making your daughter do her homework and going over it with her. Then I'm slaving over the stove cooking for y'all. I'm just in here holding it down and you come in here yelling with your old played-out pictures tellin' me to get out. I see how you do."

"I apologize, baby. Okay," she says with seductive eyes, "watch how mommy makes it up to you." She now looks me in my eyes while unzipping my pants and pulling them down. After a quick kiss she goes down on her knees and places me into her mouth. As she sensuously glides her soft lips and tongue in so many ways, I lean back against the refrigerator and enjoy the moment. A second ago she was cussing at me, now she's loving me. She makes a loud, slurping sound and pulls me out of her mouth.

"You like that, daddy?" she says looking up to me.

"I love it, mommy."

CHAPTER 16

Butter pulls up to Robin's home and blows the horn. When Robin appears Butter continues to blow the horn.

"Hold your horses. Damn!" Robin says as she walks to the passenger seat. "Is today a special day or something? Donald let you drive the truck? Aw shit! It's on tonight!"

"Girl, please," Butter says smiling. "I drive this all the time. This is *our* truck, not *his* truck."

Robin frowns. "When was the last time you drove it?"

"I drove it to work twice."

"Is that it?"

"Yup!" Both ladies start laughing very hard, then Butter speaks again. "I can take it whenever I get good and ready now."

"Since when?"

"Since I whipped Donald."

"You did what?!" Robin screamed, sat up in her seat, and focused on Butter. "Okay, give me all of the details, girl."

Butter hadn't had sex in so long that she couldn't wait to tell Robin of how she's been suddenly getting it on the regular. "Girl, we been going at it like rabbits lately. I mean all of the time at night."

"Girl, when you said you whipped him I thought you beat him up or something. The last thing that I expected was the two of you having sex. It's been so long. Okay, what happened? He was all up in his video game and hanging with his crew for the longest time. Now he's Mr. Loverman?"

"I don't know. One night someone called with good news and the next thing I knew we were going at it in the bedroom."

Robin noticed her friend's high spirits and wanted to dig deeper for more details. "Did he go down on you, yet?"

"I told you that he don't do that."

"Well, get to the good part. Then again, if he ain't go down on you then there is no good part."

"Look, stop asking me questions so I can talk." Once Robin sat quietly Butter continued. "I went down on him and –"

"But he won't go down on you?"

"Excuse me! I'm talking!"

Robin hissed as Butter continued.

"At least he did kiss me a few times and I got on top and –"

"Boring!" Robin chanted. "You used to know how to tell good, romantic, nasty, kinky stories. Since you been married your stories have been whack."

"Forget you!" Butter says laughing.

"Don't get me wrong, but you ain't had no stories since Daren, oops..." Robin turned toward her window so that Butter couldn't see her devilish smirk.

"There you go. That's alright. Donald may not be like Daren, but he's getting there. It's taking a little time, but the sex is getting better. At least he's trying new things that Daren wouldn't."

"Like what?"

"I don't know...like fingers in the butt."

"He put his fingers in your ass? That ain't nothing new. Didn't Daren do that to you a few times?"

"Yes, but he wouldn't let me do that to him."

"Him who?"

"Daren."

"You didn't do it to Daren, but -"

"But I did it to my husband."

"How many fingers?"

"Two! Dag! Why you wanna know all that?"

"Donald took two fingers in the ass?" As Robin speaks Butter begins to laugh at her question, but Robin isn't amused. "Tamela, how did y'all get into that and when?"

"About a week or so ago. We were making love and something just told me to try putting a finger in there so I did it. Robin, don't look at me like that. You told me that you read about it in Soul Mates Dissipate a year or so ago."

"I remember."

"Thank you."

"But I also told you that it was a way to find out if a man was gay or not."

"Robin, you ain't tell me that part."

"Yes, I did. Remember you tried it on Daren."

"No. I ain't never do it to him I just told you."

"I know, because when you tried it he jacked your ass up. I remember that story very well. Both of y'all told it to me and I was laughing hard as I don't know what."

"Anyway, I did that and -"

"Anyway nothin'! I ain't finished. You need to keep an eye on Donald because that motherfucka sounds gay."

"Whatever...Donald...gay?"

"Gay, homosexual, lover of dicks, penis promoter, man-humper...need I continue?"

"Robin, you ain't funny."

"Tamela, I'm being serious. He just let you go in his backdoor and he ended up taking two fingers at that? He's probably used to getting it up the ass."

"My husband ain't gay!" Butter's eyes widened as she felt a headache coming on. "Please, stop saying that, Robin."

Robin began getting angered by Butter's defensiveness. "I didn't say he was gay. I just said you need to keep an eye on him. You're my girl and I'm going to look out for you when something doesn't seem right."

"I appreciate it, but I didn't ask you for any help. Things are getting better and we were just bonding. You don't have to worry about me telling you anything else."

"Whatever!"

"Whatever then! Are you jealous?"

"Bitch, please. You ain't getting enough dick for me to be jealous! All he do is make you cry all the damn time and stress you out. You call me for advice, but now you don't want it. I see how you get. Hmph! Goin' call me jealous. Please!"

Butter didn't reply to Robin's statement. Instead, she parallel parked the truck, which took her almost ten minutes to do. Robin asked if she wanted her to help, but Butter ignored her and successfully parked the truck five minutes later. Queen Aiesha performed that night at the Comedy Club and everyone enjoyed the performance except for Butter. Robin was laughing in tears and holding her stomach, but Butter seemed unmoved. Her mind was on her husband's whereabouts and why he would cancel coming to the Comedy Club with her after she bought the two tickets far in advance. Thank goodness Robin was available at the last minute. After the show Butter stopped to drop Robin home.

"Bye, Tammy. Drive safely."

Butter rolled her eyes at her.

"Bye, Butter," Robin said with a smile and then she closed the door.

Butter rolled down the passenger window. "Robin."

"Oh, so now you can talk."

"Stop playing, Robin. Listen to me – don't tell Daren what I told you."

"Why are you bringing him up? Be concerned with your husband, girlfriend."

"Don't tell Daren."

"I love you, big head. Even if you tried to spoil all the fun at the club."

"I'm sorry, okay? That skit that Teddy Carpenter did about the girl with the retarded brother was funny. It was hard as I don't know what trying not to laugh, but I had some stuff on my mind."

"You should have some stuff on your mind. Well, I apologize for getting on you about your husband so hard in the car. It's just too easy to talk bad about him because I don't like him."

"Fuck you," Butter said.

Robin laughed and proceeded to walk away. "Bye, Tammy. Drive safely."

"Don't forget what I said."

"What?"

"Don't tell Daren what I told you."

CHAPTER 17

I've reserved the TV, bought sodas, and ordered three pepperoni pizzas for my kids. It's been pretty intense with this STAT 9 standard achievement test lingering and my students need a break from all of their hard work. As they return from Art class they immediately notice the TV and the smell of pizza and they get anxious.

"We having pizza, Mr. Brown?" asks Latisha.

"It's right in your face," yells Ernest. "Are you blind or just plain stupid?"

"Wasn't nobody talking to you. I said 'Mr. Brown,' thank you!"

Kids will argue over anything. Instead of verbally getting on them, I remain sitting quietly. Within seconds they get the message that until it gets quiet, they won't eat or enjoy the movie. The room is now quiet and I give them a quick speech on how they are being rewarded for their hard work. I send Angela to wash her hands and when she returns I give her plates to pass out to everyone. Now it's time to dismiss those that played and disrupted the class while I was teaching all year long.

"I'm tellin' you, youngin', Mr. Brown is cool as I don't know what. He's my favorite teacher, man. I'm tellin' you."

Now listen to that knucklehead, Vernon Clark. He and Marcel Garner are like Craig and Day-Day from Friday – always getting into trouble in my class and getting on my damn nerves. Vernon is trying to talk loud and say nice things because he suspects that I'm sending him to Mr. Jackson's room. No student wants to go there. They can't stand the smell of him and his room and I can't either. I'm sending Vernon, Marcel, and Andre. Rico is sitting over there trying to act like he's sleeping. I should send him to Mr. Funky's class, too.

"Vernon, Marcel, and Andre, I need a favor. I need for you to go to Mr. Jackson's class and -"

"Funky Jackson?" Vernon yells. Everyone in the class begins to laugh except for Angela.

"Anyway, I need for you three to ask Mr. Jackson to send his three students down here."

"Is Katrina coming?" asks Vernon. "Can she sit next to me?"

"Why?" I ask.

"If you see that body you'll know why," Vernon responds while raising his eyebrows up and down with a sinister look on his face.

"Bye, Vernon."

"I'm sayin' tho, Mr. Brown, she has a body like a sixth grader," he continues. "It's better than all the fourth graders in our room."

"Bye, fellas," I say pushing him out of the door. Marcel and Andre follow behind him.

Angela has finished passing out the plates and she places those remaining on my desk. "Mr. Brown, they ain't coming back, are they?"

"Ain't?"

"I mean they aren't coming back, are they? You are just trading them for three of Mr. Jackson's students?"

I can only smile at Angela's intelligence. Only she knew that Mr. Jackson is supposed to keep those three students of mine for an hour and a half. All that I have to do is send him some pizza and keep three of his students. If I had told them that they had to stay there, they would have acted a fool and caught attitudes because - "Hey! What are y'all doing over there?"

"Mr. Brown," Latisha calls out, "James is mad because someone put dandelions and buttercups in his desk and he doesn't know who did it."

James gets up and throws the "bouquet" of wild flowers in the trash. I brush off the situation to maintain order, but I know that Winston put the flowers there. I even recall him skipping away from the Double-Dutch crew to pick those flowers. I'm sure that all of the girls that were jumping rope with him know that he did it. As I look in his direction I can see him peeking at me out of the corners of his eyes. I'm about sick of him coming on to other boys.

Finally the movie is in and my kids are relaxing and enjoying themselves. I'm taking this time to grade some papers in peace, but I hear too much talking coming from a small cluster of young men. "Fellas, I need it quiet."

Rico looks up. "Marquies went to the Cash Money Millionaire's concert last night."

"Marquies, come here, please," I request. As he sits next to me I tell him to explain what happened at the show. I know he wasn't out on a school night at a concert. He's only nine-years-old anyway.

"Mr. Brown, you should have seen it. First, Eve came out and rapped. Then Lil' Wayne came out. Then DMX came out and he was barking and stuff."

"You like X?"

"X is tight. Then the Cash Money Millionairs came out and they got girls from the audience to get on stage and this one girl got up there and started dancing and she took her shirt and bra off and showed her –"

"Brrrr..." I say trying to lead him to the correct term.

"Yeah, she showed her -"

"B-r-e-a-s-t-s," I spell out for him.

"Yeah, she showed her titties."

I can't believe this boy. I try to lead him to use the correct word and I even spelled it out for him. I now take a moment to tell him the correct word and for him not to use tittie in the classroom anymore. Just then Ms.Bishop comes into the room.

"You're wanted in the office."

"Oh yeah?" What in the hell is this for?

"Yes. I'm going to watch your students.

"Help yourself to some pizza and soda," I say and make my way out of the room. I hope that Vernon, Marcel, and Andre went to Mr. Jackson's class and not to run up and down the halls instead. Once I reach the office, the secretary walks me into the principal's office where a little boy is sitting. The principal begins to speak.

"Mr. Brown, do you know this boy?"

"No." I don't have any kids. He looks around nine or ten-years-old. Who was I sexin' ten years ago? He doesn't even look like me.

"Do you recall putting your hands on him and hitting him?"

"No. I don't hit my kids."

"Well, he says you punched him."

"No, I didn't," the boy says.

"Well, his mother says you did."

"He's not one of my students. Whose class is he in?"

"Mrs. Riley's."

"I haven't been to her class. I don't know this little boy."

The secretary then returns to the principal's office. "Mr. Brown, we have a problem. See, his mother called and threatened your life. Now his uncles are outside waiting for you. They say they're going to kill you."

Looking out of the office window I see two men bouncing a basketball next to my car. What kind of shit is this? Someone has to be playing a practical joke or something. This can't be happening to me. Walking back to my class, I click into survival mode. These motherfuckas ain't goin' to kill me. I'll fight one, but not two.

"Mr. Brown!" I look back and see the janitor walking towards me. "You okay?"

"I'm cool. What's up?"

"I just talked to Mike and Tom and –"

"Those two dudes out by my car? Tell them I'll fight the big one. Can you hold the small one back for me?"

"Mr. Brown, them niccas got guns."

"Guns?"

"Yeah. This ain't back in the days when you could just fight with your fist. These young boys play for keeps. I went and tried to tell them that they were overreacting and you wouldn't hit a kid. I told them that you were cool and while Mike was dribbling the ball his

jacket flung open and a gun was there. I
think he has a .38, but I ain't sure."

What if these motherfuckas shoot me?
Ain't this a bitch? I go back into class and
stop the movie when Ms. Bishop leaves. "Take
out one sheet of paper." All that can be heard
are moans and groans. "I'll start the movie
in a second. Take out one sheet, please."
After all have done so, I give them the assignment. "Everyone, I need you to write a
paragraph about how you would feel if you
never saw Mr. Brown again after today. How
would you feel if Mr. Brown suddenly died?"

"Are you sick?" asked Arshalese.

"Are you going to die, Mr. Brown?"
Rachel asked. "Did you receive the bad news
from your doctor when you left the room?"

The results of the assignment were
touching. Alanah wrote that she loved me
and would try to come see me wherever I
went. She said that if something happened
to me she would put flowers on my grave
once a month because I was her favorite
teacher. James said that I was more important than his father whom he only sees every
blue moon. Angela said she would miss me
because I was one of the only people that
treated her like she was somebody special.
Winston burst into tears as he read his feelings, and that made many of the other students either cry or get teary eyed.

I now begin to get chills up and down
my spine because I feel the love that my

kids have for me. They need me here and there is no other place that I'd rather be. I love them, too, and I have to be here for them tomorrow and the day after.

"Mr. Brown! Come here, quickly!" came Ms. Johnson's voice. She is a fifth grade teacher down the hall from me. As I step into the hallway she tells me to get into the closet. I look at her with questioning eyes. "Mr. Brown, get in the closet and don't come out until you hear my voice!"

I do as she says because I trust her at this point. Standing in the darkness, my heart begins racing and my adrenaline is pumping. I'm ready to kick somebody's ass, but I can't beat a gun. Ten minutes later Ms. Johnson returns.

"Okay, Mr. Brown, come on out. There were two men running around looking for you. They finally left the building because they knew that the police were called, but they're still outside."

These motherfuckas are crazy! Goin' to shoot me in my class? In front of my kids? I work too hard and put up with too much shit to go out like this.

"Who are you calling?"

"I'm about to call my crew."

"They already called the police. That's why the guys left the building. The police should be here at any moment." Ms. Johnson then leaves.

Unfortunately, an hour has passed and the police haven't shown. Worse than that, none of the staff have been allowed to leave because of the two men being outside. As I walk past the lounge I hear grumbles of how everyone's upset, and I believe they are blaming me. Some probably think that I really hit that little boy. This shit ain't my fault. I don't know what this is all about. Suddenly my phone rings.

"Hello?"

"Daren, I hear you're in a little bind."

"Officer Wright? You're behind this?"

"No. I just heard about it on my police radio. I'm not behind it, but I can get you out of it. Just say you'll start seeing my wife."

"Twelve thousand, right?"

"I'll give you five thousand."

"Five? Hell no!"

"Five thousand and you get to keep your life. These boys play for keeps. I'll take care of them for you if you just agree to help me with Marcy."

"It's a deal," I surrender.

"Call her right now."

Within three minutes three police cars converge on the scene along with a paddy wagon. Mike and Tom are arrested, the teachers and staff get to leave safely, and I'm on my way to Marcy's house. I've literally dodged a bullet. Now my phone rings again.

"Yeah?"

"Daren, meet me on Southern and Wheeler. You know that old grocery store right next to the gas station? Meet me there for a second. I have something to show you."

I do as Officer Wright says. The condemned grocery store is only three blocks away from my school. I turn into the huge parking lot and see the police cars and the paddy wagon. Officer Wright waves me toward him as he leans from the back of the wagon. I park and walk over and immediately see blood on the wagon's floor.

"What's up, Brown? You want to take a few shots at these two?" Mike and Tom are slumped down in the wagon with their heads bleeding. I think Officer Wright is setting me up. "Come on up here and whip their asses for threatening to kill you."

"I ain't fuckin' with them. I just want them to know that I ain't hit their nephew. He ain't even in my classroom."

"Daren, where's your killer instinct? You are supposed to inflict some type of pain on these fools for fuckin' with you. You ain't gonna do shit, huh?" Officer Anthony then slams his foot into the side of one of their heads. The other bleeding man catches Officer Wright's nightstick across his head. "You see this man?" Officer Wright asks as he points to me. "If anything happens to him I'm going to kill both of you. Understand?" The two men nod in agony and Officer Wright backs away with his eyes still piercing at them. He then looks down to the lower half of his own body. "Shit, y'all got blood on my motherfuckin' pants!"

CHAPTER 18

Marcy didn't answer her phone, but I still drove past her house to see if she was home. I called back again and left another message before leaving. Officer Wright and I made a deal and I'm going to respect it, Especially after the jam he got me out of just now. Cops can be ruthless. He really put a hurtin' on those two dudes in the paddy wagon. I ain't scared of him or nothin', but I don't want no shit. I have enough on my plate as it is. I need a nice, cold beer right about now.

Pulling into Raquel's driveway and seeing her daughter really relieves me. Seeing her innocent little face and pretty smile makes today's drama seem less important and unworthy of too much thought.

"Hey, sweetie!" I say while slightly squatting and opening my arms to embrace her. "How was school today?" I hope your day was better than mine." She explains her day as she hugs me and I feel the life come back to my heart. Kids make problems so much easier to deal with. "Where's your homework? What assignment do you have to complete?"

"I already got started on it. Look." She reaches over to the dining room table and hands me a piece of paper.

"I sit on the sofa and begin reading her assignment and checking it. Now here she comes squeezing her body between my knees, trying to read what I'm reading. "Excuse you."

"What?" she asks smiling. "Are they right?"

"So far so good." I continue to check her multiplication. Not to toot my own horn, but toot-toot! Since I've been in the picture this little girl has made major improvements in Math and Reading. Not only that, she's beginning her homework without being asked and having better behavior in school. Lately I've had to give her a little extra homework because she's knocking her assignments out so quickly. "I'm proud of you, sweetie! You have all of them correct."

"YES!" she exclaims while lifting her arms in the air in victory. She then jumps up in my lap and gives me another hug.

"What's 9 x 7?" I blurt out.

"63," she says with a smile.

"Just checking...just checking," I say and I smile back. I guess I'll postpone my beer until Raquel gets home. For the time being, I reach for the remote control and cut on the TV so we can watch some cartoons. That's another thing Raquel's daughter loves about me; I can watch all of the new cartoons and know all of the characters and the episodes. She doesn't realize that being a teacher keeps me abreast to what kids' interests are these- "What are you doing?!" I yell as I quickly jump up off of the sofa. I can't believe that she seemed to have pulled my hand under her skirt. I look at her in shock as she stands from having fallen on the floor. Though standing, her eyes are looking down to the floor.

I can't believe this! I wonder if it's those music videos she watches or if it's those "grown" little boys at her school? It's probably those fresh little girls in the neighborhood influencing her. However, I have over four years of dealing with children and I know how to get answers out of them.

"Sweetheart, I'm not mad at you."

"Yes, you are." She now begins to cry, but her voice doesn't change. "You're going to leave."

"Sweetie, I'm not mad and I'm not going to leave." It can't be more convincing than the way I said it. "But, sweetheart, it's important that you tell me why you put my hand there. Has someone been touching you there? It's okay, sweetie. You can tell me. I won't tell anyone, not even Mommy. Has someone been touching you down there?"

"Yes."

"Who?"

"Uncle Brandon."

That dirty motherfucka! That's her father's friend. I've never met him, but Raquel can't stand him. "When did this start, sweetie?"

"Last year."

My baby is hurting inside and she has been for the past year. I should roll over to where they hang out and bust Brandon in the head my damn self. I sit down and hug her and tell her "Everything's okay," while my mind conjures up ways of hurting Brandon and how I'm going to explain it to Jesus. Brandon better hope I don't find him!

"You aren't going to tell Mommy, are you?"

Damn! Now how am I supposed to tell her this? I sure don't want to tell her over the phone. I guess I'll tell her when she gets home this evening. Brandon better hope that she doesn't catch him.

"No, I'm not going to tell Mommy, but you are."

"No!"

"You're a big girl. And no one on this earth cares about you like Mommy does. Whenever you have a problem in life you can always share it with Mommy. She'll always love you. The sooner you tell her about what's been happening the better. We don't want Uncle Brandon to hurt you anymore. Understand, sweetie?"

"Yes."

It's 8:00 PM in Raquel Patterson's home and the evening is just beginning. Daren wanted to tell Raquel about the situation with her daughter, but she began to tell him how rough her day went. All that Raquel wanted to do was eat and rest. She talked with her daughter and then the three of them ate the chicken fettucini alfredo dinner that Daren prepared. They then watched a little TV and then it was time for her daughter to take a bath.

After a hard day's work, coming home to a nice meal and not having to make her daughter do her homework was a blessing. *That's what Daren is*, she thought as she snuggled in his arms on the sofa, *a true blessing*. It was then that Daren told Raquel everything that happened at school with the threats and after school with Officer Wright. He thought that if he let her know how rough his day went it would make her stressful day at work not look so bad, and that would make the news of her daughter being molested a little easier for her to swallow.

As soon as her daughter went to sleep, Raquel planned on making some real good love to Daren since he went through so much. She couldn't imagine receiving threats on her life and then seeing the two men pummeled by the officer. Raquel began feeling selfish for bringing her little bit of stress from the job to Daren when he had much more stress than she had experienced. When her daughter left the bathroom in her pajamas and received her goodnight kisses, Raquel knew it was lovin' time.

"Goodnight, Precious," Raquel said.

"Goodnight, Mommy...goodnight, Friend."

"Goodnight, sweetie," Daren said.

Raquel loved how she could not only bring Daren around her daughter, but also how she couldn't see not having him around. He was such a positive influence on Precious and an excellent father figure.

"Daren, go get in the shower and prepare yourself to be loved very passionately and very slowly."

Daren loved the way that sounded. He postponed his beer earlier because he didn't like drinking in front of children and Raquel's order made him postpone his beer a little longer. When he disappeared into the bathroom, Raquel grabbed a jar of honey from the kitchen cabinet and stopped by her daughter's room on her way to the bedroom. She lay in bed looking at the ceiling.

"Goodnight, Precious. Mommy is so proud of how well you're doing in school."

A lump formed in Precious' throat, but she mustered up the courage to say, "Mommy, he's been touching me down here," as she pointed below her waist.

Raquel froze while her mind began to swirl in a storm of confusion and anger. In the midst of her thoughts, she kissed her daughter on the forehead as her daughter began to cry. "It's going to be okay, baby. Just go to sleep. Mommy's not mad. We'll talk about it in the morning. Just get some sleep." Raquel marched back into the kitchen and placed the honey back into the cabinet and reached for the box of grits sitting next to it. She poured them in a pot, filled it with water, and turned the flame on hi.

Daren ran the shower water, but he did not get in. He sat on the toilet lid and contemplated how he was going to call Raquel into the bathroom and tell her everything. In his mind there would be no sex, nor any other physical pleasures, only the pains of truth and betrayal. Many minutes had passed and he continued to sit there in deep thought. He decided on taking a nice shower and then delivering the news to Raquel. He took off all of his clothes and then decided that he couldn't wait any longer to tell something that he knew would break his girlfriend's heart.

"Raquel, come here, sweetie," he yelled from the bathroom. Noticing that he was naked, he grabbed his underwear and was about to put them on when Raquel stormed in the bathroom. "Hey, sweetie. Look, we need to talk." He looked up to Raquel only to get a glimpse of her slinging a pot of hot grits in his direction.

Still sitting down, he turned his right shoulder to avoid the scalding hot liquid weapon and some of the grits stuck to his shoulder, arm, and his back while the majority of it splashed against the wall above the toilet. "Ahhhhh shit! What the fuck are you doing?!" Daren reached over and swatted the pot out of Raquel's hand and it hit the floor. He then leaned to his right and tried to let the shower water get the grits off of his body. The water only added pain to his burned flesh.

Raquel grabbed the pot off of the floor and flung what little grits remained in the pot at Daren. "You gonna die tonight, motherfucka! I hate you!" After realizing that no more grits remained in the pot she began to swing it at Daren as he attempted to rinse off the grits. "I'm a kill your ass, you fuckin' pervert!" Raquel said as the pot clunked against Daren's bald head.

Daren tried to ignore the burning sensation across his arm, shoulder, and back and focused on getting the pot out of Raquel's hand. His head felt the pain of the solid blow that he took only seconds ago, but he would get over it. As the water splashed he yanked the pot from Raquel and dropped it. Before he could try to grab her, she began throwing punches at him. The last thing that he wanted to do was punch Raquel, so he jumped out of the shower as the punches continued and he slipped on the wet floor. He grabbed his pants, stood up, and then pushed her so that he could get to the door.

Raquel fell back against the shower wall and nearly hit her head. As the water now splashed directly on her, she wiped her eyes and went after Daren who had left the room. She looked down the hall to her right and saw Daren struggling to put his pants on. She ran as fast as she could and kicked him in his right hip. She then ran into the kitchen.

The momentum from Raquel's kick made Daren hit the wall next to the front door. He maintained his balance, but he was unable to put on his pants. He tried to put his left foot into the pants when he heard the utensil drawer open. The sound of Raquel shuffling around in the drawer caught his attention so he unlocked the door and ran to his car in his underwear and bare feet. He held his pants with his left hand and searched his pockets for his car keys with his right. As he got to the door of his car Raquel came running out of the house wielding an eight-inch knife. Daren unlocked the door with his car remote and jumped in.

Raquel tried to open the driver door, but Daren had already locked it. As the car began to back down her driveway, Raquel attempted slashing the moving tires but failed. She then ran to the end of the driveway and grabbed a brick and threw it as hard as she could and cracked the rear passenger window. She stood in the street watching Daren's lights getting smaller and smaller as he drove away at top speed.

CHAPTER 19

The past couple of months have been hard as hell. The day after all of that nonsense with Raquel and the hot grits, my principal called to inform me that I was on administrative leave with pay. It really bothers me that I wasn't able to say good-bye to all of my students...all of my children. I've been missing them – James, Winston, Latisha, my sweet Alanah, Vernon, and Angela. I've been considering a different profession because teachers aren't paid shit, especially not enough to have to deal with all of the bullshit that you have to go through. Now, being on administrative leave with pay and my overall employment situation is the least of my concern.

Every hour since leaving Raquel's house she has called me with her threats. "Daren, you're going to pay for what you did to my daughter, you worthless motherfucka! I hope you suffer for what you did. And I'll bet you did hit that little boy at your school. Those men should have killed you." That's just the most recent message that she left on my voicemail. I didn't entertain shit that she said because I was too busy getting these minor burns taken care of.

Her little threats didn't bother me, but when I woke up two mornings later I discovered that I had four flat tires, and all of my car windows were busted. I was mad at that point because I had just gotten that rear window fixed the day before and then she goes and busts all of them. On top of that, she spray-painted "child molester" on each side of my car and on the hood. Getting my car towed and repainted cost me over a thousand dollars that I really didn't have to waste. I feel like killing her ass. I immediately packed a few bags of clothing and moved into a cheap hotel, and that's where I am now. I don't have to worry about Raquel's calls or having my car vandalized.

However, upon one of my mailbox visits after two weeks of being on the run, I received notice that Raquel had pressed charges against me, and that there was a warrant out for my arrest. She was also suing me. On top of that, when I went upstairs to my apartment I could tell that Officer Wright had been in there going through my stuff. Nothing was taken, but everything was all over the place as if someone was looking for something. I haven't been back there since that day.

Now Officer Wright is mad as hell because I haven't been following his orders and dating his wife. He's also mad because he can't find me. He left me a few messages telling me to contact him or else. I didn't want to appear anywhere at that point because of the Raquel situation and the warrant that was out on me.

I know the manager here at the hotel very well and he not only gave me a nice discount, but he allowed me to register my room under the name "Beverly Thomas." However, I know that I can't hide from Officer Wright for long. There goes my phone.

"Hello?"

"Mr. Brown, how are you? This is your principal Mrs. Harper."

She always speaks so eloquently and professionally. Even in the summer time. "I'm doing fine. And yourself?"

"I'm doing splendid. Mr. Brown, your students got pretty good test scores. I am very impressed. You did a marvelous job with them, but I'm not surprised because I hire smart."

Listen to her toot her own horn. Even when she's complimenting someone she still finds a way to pat herself on the back.

"Mr. Brown, the investigation of your case has concluded. It turns out that the parent wanted to have her son transferred to your class. I declined it because it was too late in the school year, and that's when the mother became livid and made up that story about you. You're free to work next school year."

"That's good. Thank you for informing me."

"Okay, Mr. Brown. If you need anything over the summer just call me at the school."

"Okay. Thank you. Get some rest this summer. Take care." I ain't never workin' with kids no more. Teaching can kiss my ass! I almost got shot over one kid and later the same day I got hot grits poured on my ass. I have to find another way to make money. Let me hurry up and get dressed so I can go jogging at Laurel Lake. Exercising is one of the few things that clears my mind and helps me think. Dag, there's my phone again. "Yo."

"Yo? Is that how we answer the phone now? Yo? You're too old for that, Daren."

"Robin! What's up, girl? How have you been?"

"Daren, don't even try to act like you're happy to hear my voice. Don't even try it."

"I am happy to hear from you. You my girl."

"Evidently I ain't your girl because you ain't called me since I don't know when. I ain't heard from you since around the time of Tammy's wedding when you came and ran off with my little sister."

"See, now why you wanna go there? We ain't even been on the phone for a minute and you're startin' trouble. Robin, you my girl and I love you, and I'm just going through some drama right now so let's be peaceful."

"Join the party. There's a lot of drama going around."

"I mean some real drama."

"Real drama? Do you need me to do anything for you, Daren? Now that I think about it, you don't sound like yourself."

"I just have some thinking to do."

"Well, let me know if you need any help. I have someone to cheer you up."

"Who? Your sister Ebony?"

"No! And before you decide to fulfill another fantasy of hers, take a cold shower or masturbate or something. I'm not playing with you, Daren Brown!" Robin begins to chuckle upon hearing Daren's laughter.

"Okay, okay. Who do you have to cheer me up?"

"Around here turning people out on planes and stuff. Anyway, I want you to let my boyfriend cheer you up."

"You got a man?"

"Why is that so hard to believe?"

"It's not, but I don't want to talk to him."

"Sure you do, Daren. Just do me this favor. Trust me. He'll make you feel better."

"I don't want to talk to no damn man, Robin."

"Daren, just do it. Dag! Trust me on this one."

"Alright, only because you my girl. But if he starts preachin' some TD Jakes stuff, I'm hanging up."

"He won't, silly. Hold on. Sweetie!" Robin calls out, "Come and get the phone." I then hear a voice that makes me smile.

"Hello?"

"What's up, Billy?"

"Hey, Loco!"

"How are you doing? Are you being good? Are you listening to your mother?"

"Yeah, Loco."

"What?"

"I mean, yes, Loco."

"That's better. How are you doing in school? Are you making good grades?"

"Yes."

"Have you been in any trouble at school?"

"Huh?"

"Have you been in trouble? Has the teacher had to call your mother?"

"She called my daddy once, but he's gone now."

"Gone?" I hope William didn't get shot or something. PG County, MD is pretty rough. "Where is he?"

"In jail. Can you take me to see him?"

"I don't know if I can. Put Robin back on the phone. I'll find a way to make sure you see him. Okay?"

"Okay. When are you going to take me to a baseball game?"

"I'll make sure that you go to a game next season."

"Okay! Bye, Loco."

"Daren?"

"Robin, what's going on?"

"Like I said earlier, there's a lot of drama going on. Don't repeat what I tell you. If this comes up later I'm a kick your butt."

"I ain't going to say nothing."

"I'm serious, Daren. You better not say one word to nobody."

"I won't. Damn. You know I'm good with keeping secrets."

"Okay, well, Tammy and Donald are not getting along at all. He don't know how to treat Billy and he's always out until early in the morning talking about he's at work. I keep telling her that don't nobody work that much. He don't even have sex with her really. Anyway, the teacher called Tammy and told her about this assignment that Billy did and...."

I can't believe all of the stuff that Butter is going through. I hope that things get better with her marriage. Robin went on to tell me that Billy hasn't done any work since his father's arrest and now he has to take summer school to pass to the next grade. His teacher said all that he does in summer school is either stare into space or sketch drawings in his notebook. I definitely can't let him stay back in school. Damn, just when

I say I ain't never workin' with kids anymore, I find a reason to start liking them. Let me drive down to Upper Marlboro and talk with Billy's father. I haven't seen him since high school, and even back then we weren't friends, but his son needs a little inspiration to do his schoolwork, so hopefully I can help somehow.

CHAPTER 20

Sitting on the other side of this thick glass, I patiently await William Walker's presence. After signing all of these papers and waiting ten minutes, the door finally opens. The timer starts and William picks up the phone. He stands at about 5'9", dark complexion, with a decent build.

"Oh shit. What you doin' comin' to see me?"

"Came to talk business. You know I use to kick it with Tamela, right?" I say looking into his eyes.

"When? Back in high school?"

"Naw, back in the late 90's."

"I ain't know that shit."

"Your son ever mention the name 'Loco'?"

"That was you? He still brings the name up every now and then. He has been for years now. What's that got to do with anything?"

"I just talked to him and Robin and she tells me he stayed back in school this year and he's about to fail summer school. He's stressed because you're in here and he won't do no work."

"He was doing good, man. That dude that Tamela married just be trippin'. They got a restraining order on me so it was hard to see my son. I was going to crack her husband's head open, and then I got locked up over some dumb shit that I ain't even do."

"I'm about to get you out of here. What's your bail?"

"It was 50 thousand, but that damn policeman found a way to make it a hundred thousand."

"Damn! That shit sounds personal. That's ten thousand to get you out."

"My crew got three grand and I got two. I just need five grand. If you got that I'll get that shit back to you. Just get me out of here."

"It's done. Just give me the number to your crew and we'll try to get you out today."

"Straight up? Well, hurry up before Officer Wright adds on some more charges. I can't stand that motherfucka."

"Did you say Officer Wright? Officer Anthony Wright?"

"Yeah. You know him?"

"Call me the second you get out. We really need to talk some business." I leave and as I make my way to my car I can smell the roses in my mind. Things are really looking better for me all of a sudden.

CHAPTER 21

I told William to meet me here at Starbucks on East-West Highway near PG Plaza. It's ten minutes before six and he's pulling up. Good. The brotha is a man of his word for showing up, and I know he's about business because he's punctual. Ever since Marcy gave me the name and address of the woman our favorite policeman is dating, I've been conjuring up a way to get him off my back. I think William's situation and my own situation will be straight if we implement my plan to a tee.

"What's up, Will?" I ask as I give him some dap and a shoulder bump.

"Everything is cool now that I'm out of there. Thanks for looking out for me. I don't ever want to be locked up anymore. So what's the deal?"

"Hold on. Are you having anything to drink? Just tell her what you want."

"I don't fuck with coffee or none of that shit. I want some real food. I've been eatin' that jail shit for months. I just got out not long ago, and I couldn't grab nothin' to eat 'cause I ain't have no money."

"Is Popeyes or Sbarro's alright with you?"

"Hell motherfuckin' yeah!"

Less than five minutes later we're sitting in the food court of PG Plaza Mall, which is right across the street from Starbucks. He's eating like he hasn't eaten in days, while I munch on some fries.

"So you know the policeman that locked me up?" William asks.

"Yeah, I know him, or should I say that he knows me and I'm trying to learn more about him?"

"What in the fuck did you just say?"

"He wants to get even with his wife and he wanted my help. I wouldn't so now he's threatening me and those around me. I didn't know that he locked you up."

"Yeah, he did! I was schemin' on Tamela's husband when Wright crept up on me and put the gun to my head. Man, he planted crack and a gun in my car. Now I have drug and weapons charges. I know I'm going to get some time in jail after I go to court for this shit."

"You may not have to if you play your cards right. I got a plan that will help both of us."

"I got a plan, too."

"Break it down."

"Me and my crew are going to follow him after my preliminary court date. Once he gets to a certain place where ain't many people around, we're going to pull up next to his car and blast his ass! If he pulls over to go into a store or something, that will make it even easier."

Although he looks satisfied with his plan, I know that it won't work. Besides, I saw his crew when I collected his half of the bail money and they don't look too smart.

What is good about his plan is the part about shooting Officer Wright. Although I am a little thrown off by how ruthless he can be, I wasn't going to shoot him. I don't wish death on any man, but after witnessing him whipping those two dudes in the back of that wagon, I know that he can easily hurt me just as quickly. I don't want to give him that chance. With William helping and doing the dirty work, he will be off my back forever.

"William, the fewer people that are in on shooting Officer Wright the better; so leave your boys out of it. Plus, if you do it after your first court hearing, they will link the killing back to you real quick. I know where this fool goes to get his freak on and it's the perfect place to get him."

"Where?"

"Up on Sheriff Road and Eastern Avenue."

At my words, William begins to smile. "There's always a million motherfuckas outside all of the time. That sounds good to me. What's your plan?"

Sounds like he's in it already. "We're going to get up in her apartment and wait for him to show up. When he does, we take care of our problem on the spot."

William then looks me dead in my eyes with the seriousness of an assassin. "Who's going to pull the trigger?"

"You just said you would when you told me your plan," I say while looking into his eyes with mine being just as serious. I'm definitely not going to kill anyone, especially not a policeman. I believe that you can get an automatic life in prison term for murdering a cop. It's bad enough that I'm an accessory, but at this point I think it's either his life or mine. "Here's what I'm thinking, Tamela's husband knows Officer Wright. He knew you were coming for him for disrespecting your son, so he called Officer Wright to take care of you. That's why he planted all that shit in your car."

I notice William's face transforming into an expression that says some of his questions are finally being answered. "Forget what I put up to bail you out," I continue. "Just handle the trigger part. I'll do my part by dropping the money you owe me. I'll put the plan in motion and I'll bring you face to face with Officer Wright."

"I need something else."

Oh shit! Here we go. Motherfuckas always want to get greedy and start asking for shit. "Something else like what?" I ask with a raised brow.

"I need you to get the restraining order lifted. I want to see my son."

"I don't know any policemen."

"You know Tamela. Do you think she'll listen to you?"

"It's worth a try."

"Here's her number."

"Call her now?" I didn't plan on talking to Butter. It's been a long time.

"Yes, call her now. I miss my son."

Before I know it, I've dialed Tamela's number...Butter's number. I now hear a rude voice on the other end.

"Tamela speaking?"

"How in the world have you been? Is this Butter?" There's nothing but silence on the other end. "Butter? Hello?"

"Why are you calling me?"

"I don't mean any disrespect."

"No, I didn't mean it like that. I just didn't expect it to be you," she says with happiness radiating through her voice.

"Well, who were you expecting?"

"Anyone but you. How have you been?"

"I've been fine. Where's your husband?"

"He sure ain't here with me smiling and giggling like this. I can't believe you called! Why you call me?"

"Where's Billy?"

"Right here."

"Let me talk to him."

"No! I have enough drama in my house. If Billy brings your name up I'll never hear the end of it."

"I just want to tell him I have tickets to a game for him."

"Who's going to take him? Not you."

"Your husband can take him."

"That will never happen."

"Why not?"

"I can't say."

"Then you take him."

"I can't. When is the game?"

"Butter -"

"Stop calling me that!"

I can tell that she's smiling. "Butter, stop being difficult and put Billy on the phone. I'll tell him to keep it a secret."

"Hold on."

"Hello?"

I quickly give the phone to William. They talk for a minute and all of a sudden William gives the phone back to me.

"Hello?"

"Daren?"

"Yeah, what's up?"

"Why in the world did he call you daddy? Did you tell him to call you that?"

"No. That's him being silly. He's probably just happy to talk to me."

"Uh-huh! Anyway, how do I get the tickets? I can't come pick them up."

"I'll give them to Robin or something and she can give them to you."

"Or you can give them to Ebony and she can give them to Robin to give to me."

"That's messed up."

"What? I ain't say nothing."

"You ain't funny. But, look, I need a favor."

"What?"

"Your son has been acting up in school, right?"

"A little. Why? Who told you that?"

"You know I'm a teacher and I know people in the system. I've been keeping track of Billy's studies through them. I think I know why he's not doing well...I need you to lift the restraining order on his father."

"Why does that concern you?"

"Your son concerns me."

"And?"

"And I think he'll do better if he knows his father is safe and if he could see him. That will probably stop him from rebelling against your husband, too."

"You talked to Robin, didn't you?"

"You just told me that you had drama in your house and that your husband would never take your son to a game."

"Oh yeah. That's right."

"Plus, William is in jail so why do you need a restraining order?"

"How did you know that?"

"The streets talk, sweetie. You know

this is a small world. Just drop the restraining order."

"Well, if he's in jail then it doesn't matter if there's an order or not. Right?"

Damn. She got me there. "But if you
drop it then he can at least see his son during visiting hours. Just do this for me, please.
I need you to do this."

"I'll think about it, although it's weird
that you're calling me."

"I'll make sure he pays you all of the
back child support that he owes you."

"Don't play!"

"I'm not playing. Drop the order and
you'll get paid. That back child support that
William owes you is real high, ain't it?" I look
over to William and he's smiling while giving
me a "fuck you" expression.

"He's in arrears about fifteen thousand.
You get me that money and I'll drop the restraining order and do anything else you want
me to."

"Okay, watch your mouth," I say laughing. "But, look, I need you to drop the order
now."

"What's the rush?"

"Just do it."

"And I'm supposed to trust you?"

"Yes. Have I ever failed you?"

"That's a good point. Okay, Daren. I'll
drop it as soon as I can. I'll call them either
today or tomorrow."

We say our goodbyes and get off the
phone. "William, it's done, playa."

"Playa nothin'," William says still smirking. "What the fuck you bring up back child support for? And where am I going to get all that money when I couldn't even get bail money? You got money like that?"

"Hell no. I ain't got no $15,000!"

"She said I owe her $15,000? Damn, it's that high?"

I smile at his question because he's looking so confused. "Look, we'll cross that bridge when we get there. You needed to get the restraining order lifted and I took care of that. Let's go over the plan that I have in detail so we can get this fool out of the way first."

For the juicy details of this chapter,

grab your copy of

Twilight Moods

and read

"Shar-Baby."

CHAPTER 22

I'm out here at Laurel Lake on a nice night just jogging and thinking. There's just so many things happening in my life and the drama serves as a wake up call. I really need to get myself together.

Meeting with William was cool –strange, but cool. We got a lot of business to take care of. I hope that Butter hurries up and drops the restraining order so he can see Billy. I really need his mind to be straight so that he can take care of Officer Wright; that way I can live in peace. If he threw William in jail and bloodied those two dudes in that wagon, there ain't no telling what he'd do to me.

Now look at this pretty young lady. I am going to make it my business to meet her tonight because I always see her out here, but I never say anything to her. She's looking good with her white tank-top, orange shorts, and white and orange Nikes.

"Welcome to my lake," I say as I approach.

"It's late and I'm really not in the mood to meet anyone or to talk. Keep walking and mind your business."

I'm not trying to push up on her, but good conversation prevails. We end up sitting together and talking about her troubled love life. While putting Off! on her pretty, caramel legs, she describes a few of the characteristics of her relationship. It's clear in my mind that her boyfriend's mental and emotional abuse is destroying her self-esteem. He's probably seeing another woman, too. I'll share my thoughts with her.

"Well..." her legs are looking so nice, "your challenge is to find out if he is taking you for granted or has just plain lost interest in you. Being taken for granted can be fixed, but once he loses interest, then chances are your relationship is over."

"That's deep, but I'm just tired. I'm tired of having to work so hard on my end and not having him return the love. He criticizes way too much and I'm just tired. You know something, it's funny how he never takes me out, but he's always out with his friends."

"Well, Sharlene, love doesn't come easy. It takes work."

"I know."

"It's nice to have finally talked to you. Good luck with your man," I say as I stand from sitting on her car.

"You're leaving already? Don't forget your Off!"

"I know you'll be back out here soon so keep it to protect those pretty legs next time."

"Thank you," Sharlene says blushing.

I returned to Laurel Lake late last night to enjoy the peaceful feeling that the water gives to me. It dawned on me then that not only has the lake been my lover, because it's been so long since I had sex, but also that I've been sneaking around at night to avoid potentially being seen by Officer Wright. I'm like a damn vampire. Anyway, while I was out there, Sharlene came back out to talk. We got into deep details about her relationship and whether or not her man was cheating. Since she seems like a genuinely nice young lady, and Lord knows she's sexy, I told her to return home and give her man all of her love. Just call me the love doctor.

I guess things didn't go too well because here she is back at the lake at 7 AM. I walk closer to her car to discover that dried tears vandalize her cheeks. They bear witness to Sharlene's pain and they attempt to hide her beauty. I can't let her spirit die. I tap on the window to wake her up.

"Step out of the car," I command.

She looks at me, unlocks the door, and attempts to check herself in the mirror. I really don't have time for the physical because her soul needs healing. I open the door and pull her out and into my arms.

"Come get this love, sweetie," I say as I gently squeeze and caress her. I don't let go until I think of how to fix her situation. Damn, she feels good. It's been so long since I've held a woman.

This morning I took Sharlene to the spa to raise her spirits and her morale. I got her a manicure, pedicure, and I got her hair done at the same time. I even got involved and massaged her feet while the three women were working on her. I've never seen a woman smile so hard. She was so happy that I got her a facial afterwards. She's back at my hotel now while I'm out here getting us some food. That's probably her calling me now.

"Hello?"

"Daren, wait, don't hang up!"

Shit! It's Raquel. I haven't answered any of her calls since the grits, but I forgot to check the caller ID just now. "What's up?"

"Daren, I was so wrong and I'm sorry. Please believe me. I know that it wasn't you that molested my daughter. She was scared, but she finally told me the truth about her father's friend. She told me everything including the talk y'all had. Daren, I am so sorry. I need to see you."

"Did you drop the charges against me?"

"Yes, and I'm sorry for that, too. I'm sorry for the grits, for messing up your car, and for calling you with all of those threats."

"I accept your apology. You really fucked my mind up, but I accept your apology."

"Thank you, baby. Thank you so much. Can you come over?"

"For what, Raquel?"

"I have some more apologizing to do. Maybe I'll cook you a nice dinner or take you out somewhere. I don't know. I just want to make up with you. Plus, my daughter misses you. She's been sad since the first day you stopped coming over. She was even .mad at me for a while."

"She heard everything that night, didn't she?"

"Unfortunately, she did. That's why she didn't want to tell me the truth because she was scared of what she thought I would do to her. We eventually had a talk and she's getting better. I have found her crying a few times; she's really attached to you."

"I'm attached to her, too. Precious is a sweetheart. I love her like she's my own." My food is ready so I grab it and head out of the restaurant to my car. "Okay, well, let me go."

"Are you coming over?"

"No."

"No? Will you at least consider coming over one day soon so I can apologize for all of that nonsense I caused? I feel so bad."

"I gotta go, but do you have some money to pay for the damage to my car?"

"How much did it cost? I can get some money to you."

The first thing I notice when I walk through the door of my hotel room is a skeptical look across Sharlene's face. "What's up, Shar?"

"Daren, why are you doing this? Why the breakfast, spa treatment, ice cream, and Chinese food? Why?"

Here we go. She was cool all morning and afternoon at the spa. Now she's questioning everything. She must have been on the phone talking to one of her girlfriends. "I'm doing this to celebrate."

"Celebrate what?"

"This morning you felt like life wasn't worth living. Like love didn't love you, right? Well, you and I are celebrating a new you. A better you. How do you feel after all you've experienced today?"

"I feel wonderful. I feel great."

"And that's how you should always feel. You only live once and your time is precious, so if a man doesn't bring you even half of the joy I've brought you, then he aint' worth your time. You were treated like a queen today and that's how you should see yourself. That's how I see you." I notice that tears are swelling in Shar's eyes. "Tears of joy?" I ask with a whisper.

"Yes," she whispers back.

I lean toward her and softly lick the tears from her left eye's stream. "It's been more than two months since you had sex?"

"Yes," she says and I feel her body beginning to quiver with anticipation.

"Well, how long has it been since you had someone make love to you?" I ask as I kiss her neck and shoulders and eventually pick her up and make her straddle my lap.

"Kiss me, Daren. I need you to kiss my lips."

After a premium sex session I realize that I haven't had a love making experience like that in a long time. Oh, we had so much fun! After that episode we chatted for a little while and she told me her fantasy was to make love outside. Ha! Right down my alley. I told her that we were going to get some ice cream, but I actually planned on taking her to a nice park and making love again.

When we first got here, I started kissing on her and the daggone police came and flashed a light into the woods near where we were. I grabbed her hand and took her deeper into the woods because I know the police won't come back here. She's now sucking my dick and it's feeling so good.

Ri-i-i-i-ing

Dag! It's her cell phone and she sounds a little upset at the voice on the other end. I think it's the father of her children. After listening a little longer I know it's her children's father. Let me put myself back in my drawers and zip my zipper before these mosquitoes get any ideas. I wouldn't want for them to hurt themselves since I'm so hard.

"Daren, I gotta go."

"It's alright. You don't have to explain anything to me." We walk back down the path and the police car is still parked there, but now his lights are out. The closer that I get I notice that it's a DC squad car. It's Officer Wright! This motherfucka is crazy! He's in PG County, Maryland with a DC police car. He's way out of his jurisdiction.

Officer Wright had his gun ready and was about to jump out of his car and shoot Daren when he noticed another person in the area. He paused to analyze the scene and realized that Daren had another woman. *I'm going to kill this fool! He's lucky she's here. I ought to kill both of them,* Officer Wright thought to himself.

As Sharlene gets into the car we pull away and I continue to look in my rearview to see if I'm being followed. I'm trying to be cool in front of Sharlene, but this fool is crazy. I think that I came close to dying back there. I drop Sharlene off where we parked her car and I immediately call William.

"Ay, it has to go down tonight. Meet me at the recreation center on Addison Road and Martin Luther King."

CHAPTER 23

Daren, also known as Mr. Blue, and William, also known as Mr. Black, walked through the apartment building wearing all black clothing. They kept their skullcaps in their pockets and each had a gun tucked in his waist. William brought Daren a gun just in case. When they got to the correct door, they put on their skullcaps and Daren forced his credit card through the doorsill and bumped the door with his hip with one powerful bump. The lights were out and Daren stepped all of the way in and reached for the light. When the light switch was flicked, Daren found himself staring at a gun.

"Don't move, motherfucka, or I will bust your ass!" says a very attractive young woman. She appears to be in her early 20's with a youthful toned body. She stands 5'6" and she has a beautiful almond complexion. Although she stays in the hood, the men there gawk over her and never get the opportunity to date her. She has too much class to be bothered with them.

Daren doesn't say a word. He just slowly puts his hands in the air. The woman reaches over to close the door without taking her eyes off of Daren and suddenly feels someone grab her arm and she hears a gun cock.

"Don't you move, bitch! Where's your man?" says William.

"Fuck! I knew this would happen. Look, please, don't shoot me. I got a son in here and I'll do anything to protect him. Just don't shoot me?"

"Shut up! What's your name?"

"Nia. My son is in the next room. What do y'all want?"

"I just asked you where's your man." William looked up and saw Daren come out from searching the back room.

"He ain't here," says Daren.

"I know, Blue, she's about to tell us where he is."

"I don't know where he is and he ain't my man. He did call and say he was coming here tonight. Sometimes he stays here, sometimes he don't."

"Nia," Daren says, "why are you pulling guns on people? What are you hiding?"

"I was protecting my son."

"You're protecting more than that. Tie her up, Black. She's lying to protect her boyfriend."

"Okay, okay! I thought y'all were coming to rob us."

"Rob y'all? You just said he wasn't your man, right? You better talk fast because we don't have no patience, Nia. Don't fuck around. We ain't here to play."

"Look, can y'all let me go? Please, don't hurt me."

"You better talk fast. He just told you that we ain't playing," says William.

"Okay, I'm not protecting Anthony, I'm protecting me and my son. Anthony keeps his drugs here from his arrests and drug busts."

"Where's that shit at?" William asks. "Is it some here now?"

"Yes, in the bedroom closet."

Daren runs to the back and returns. "Black, there's a lot of shit in there. Go look." William leaves the room and then he returns and smiles at Daren. "Okay, Nia, when is he coming here?"

"He called and said that he'd be here tonight? Y'all didn't come to rob us?"

"No, but we are now. We just came here to kill your boyfriend," said William. Daren looked at him like he was crazy.

"Look, explain everything, Nia, so nobody gets hurt." Daren says. "If you keep your mouth closed you may live."

Nia continued to explain that Officer Wright arrested her sister more than a year ago and left her broke with nowhere to turn.

Officer Wright came to her with the offer of letting him crash there when he wanted to rest. He eventually began moving drugs into her apartment and selling them in bulk to drug dealers. He promised Nia that he would help get her sister out of jail and she had been waiting a long time for him to keep his word. Lately she had come to the realization that he was lying, but she didn't know how to get rid of him now that he was paying all of her bills and also making her an accessory to his criminal actions.

CHAPTER 24

Butter was happy to have some peace and quiet. Her husband wasn't home with her, but at least there wasn't any bickering and arguing between him and Billy. That was the only positive from the situation. She really loved the comfort of a man, but lately that comfort came at the cost of lots of drama, which didn't allow any peace within the home.

She took her time and pulled the big clothes hamper into the kitchen. She thought about how long they'd been living in the apartment and how Donald never talked about moving into the house that he spoke of back when they got married. *At least we have an apartment with a full-sized washer and dryer*, she thought. She had to remain positive to keep her sanity.

As Butter started the washer and sorted the clothes she began to think about the honeymoon that she never received. The closest outing that she got was that trip to the movie theatre that night. She felt insulted, unappreciated, and taken for granted, but she didn't want to bring up her feelings to Donald because she was sure that an argument would ensue.

She put in a couple of scoops of detergent and then decided to put in another half of cup since she was also washing some of Donald's basketball gear with that load. She then began checking pockets. *What if I find something in his pockets that explains where he's been late at night? What if I find some phone numbers?* Butter checked his pockets before, but this time felt strange, almost as if she knew she'd find a clue that Donald had been messing around. She checked two pair of his gym shorts and found nothing. When she got to the last pair she took a deep breath, closed her eyes, and reached in the first pocket. Nothing there. She then took a deep breath, closed her eyes, and reached into the other pocket. Nothing again.

Butter exhaled. Her suspicions did not pan out and she was happy that they didn't, but in a way she was upset. She felt that if she found a phone number or a letter that it would at least give her an explanation of why her husband wasn't too interested in her and why he would disappear at times. She put the thoughts to the side and continued putting clothes in the washer.

"Uuugh..." she shrieked as she picked up a pair of Billy's underwear. "I know that I taught him to wipe himself better than this."

Butter sprayed the brown streak in the underwear and realized that they belonged to Donald, not Billy. Upon further examination, she noticed that the streak was more like a smudge and not only that, the smudge was in the inside of the front of the under-wear, not in the rear. "I can't stand a triflin' man." Butter kept a bitter frown on her face and put the underwear in the trash.

CHAPTER 25

Within minutes, "Mr. Blue" and "Mr. Black" pack the bags of money into larger trash bags and head for the open window in the living room so they can leave. Their cars are a block down Sheriff Road heading west. They both climb out and are impossible to see in the dark shadows with their dark clothing.

"Black," Daren pauses, "give me your bag. It doesn't take two of us to go to the car. Plus, one of us needs to be watching Nia and packing all of that coke."

William tried to look into Daren's eyes to see if they reflected trust. It was impossible due to the darkness so he went with the idea. Daren wouldn't leave without accomplishing the goal of offing Officer Wright, and if he did, William would have all of the cocaine in the apartment, which was worth much more than the bags of money.

"Okay, Blue. Handle that, and I'll go pack the coke." William extended his bag to Daren and ran back to the open window and climbed in.

Daren put the bags in the trunk nonchalantly as if they were nothing more than bags of dirty laundry in hopes that any watching eyes wouldn't get curious. He then walked back to the window and before he could climb inside, Mr. Black was handing him three plastic grocery bags full of kilos of cocaine.

"Take these, Blue, and hurry back. There is another bag of this and a couple bags of sticky green."

"Weed?" Daren asks. "Man, leave that."

"Blue, this is a robbery, right? We takin' everything including the weed and the guns. Now hurry up before someone sees us."

Daren walked to the car, put the bags in the trunk and started the engine. He was extremely paranoid now and he knew that robbers sometimes got robbed while robbing. He drove the car around the block and back and parked closer to the apartment window. He put on his hazard lights and went back to the window where William was waiting.

"Blue, what took you so fuckin' long? Let's get this shit over with. Take these." William handed Daren three bags this time. "Ain't nothin' left but some guns."

Officer Anthony Wright was coming down the hall to Nia's apartment with hopes

of getting some rest and relaxation. He had
a bottle of Hennessy, a 20-piece bucket of
Popeye's Chicken, and a pack of Dutch Mas-
ters. It would be just him and Nia alone tonight just kickin' it. He knew that he had
been rough and disrespectful to her lately
because he was stressed from not being able
to find Daren, so he felt he had to give her
some extra attention.

The plan was to make her feel special
from day one so he could stash his drugs
there while he searched for buyers. It was
bad enough that he had gotten her sister
arrested and locked away in jail so he would
promise her that, in due time, he would get
her released. Since Nia loved her sister so
much she readily agreed with whatever Anthony suggested. He wanted to make her
feel like she was a partner in crime so she
would feel just as guilty as he was, that way
he didn't have to worry much about her
snitching to the police. However, lately he
had been neglecting her so he now had a
two-person party planned, and also $200 for
her to go shopping for her son. Hopefully this
would buy him another month or two of her
time and space.

Opening the door to Nia's apartment,
Officer Wright looked up to see William standing there holding three grocery bags. "What
the fuck?!" Officer Wright yelled while dropping his bags and drawing his gun from his
waist.

The sound of the front door opening was never heard by William because of the sound of his own footsteps walking from the bedroom to the living room. Hearing Officer Wright's voice, he immediately dropped the bags and broke for the bedroom where he mistakenly left his gun. Reaching the hallway in two quick strides, William ducked down as three bullets blasted from Officer Wright's gun and tore massive holes into the walls barely missing him.

"You gangsta, nicca? Huh? Up in my spot? Nicca, you gonna die tonight!" At that moment Officer Wright checked his gun and discovered he only had one bullet left. He decided to use it to intimidate William. "I should have just killed you when I locked you up!" he yelled while firing his last bullet into the bedroom door. He hoped this would keep William in the room, which would give him time to run to his car to get more bullets. He saw Nia's legs on the floor behind the sofa. He didn't bother seeing if she was okay, he just left the apartment.

William, upon the bullet blasting through the door, grabbed his gun and escaped through the bedroom window. His plan was to surprise Officer Wright by shooting him through the living room window that he and Daren were using to take the bags from the apartment. Creeping outside of the apartment he quickly put the barrel in the window, but there was no sign of his target. Suddenly he saw something moving from the right side of the room and he aimed.

"Wait!" Nia yelled while staring into the barrel of William's gun. "He's gone," and she frantically waved her arms pointing to the door.

"Where did he go?"

"He's probably gone to his car. He always parks around the corner on the next street by the Dialysis Center!"

William ran in the direction that Nia pointed as fast as he could. He had tasted death before and, under the present circumstances, he desperately wanted to taste it again. He had no problem taking a life if it would bring him closer to his son and take him further from jail. William's life had been a living hell since the day he was arrested by Officer Wright.

Daren walked the bags to the car and placed them in the trunk. As he slammed it closed, he heard four gunshots and flashes of light from the apartment. Daren ducked down, jumped back in the car, and parked it on 52nd Street. He then began running back to the apartment window and noticed that he could literally hear his heartbeat.

William ran around the corner at top speed without losing a step. The adrenaline that his blood pumped made him feel like he could run forever. While turning the corner he realized that he didn't know what kind of car Officer Wright drove, but when he noticed a parked car with the trunk open, he aimed his gun and pulled the trigger, immediately pumping two shots into the trunk.

Officer Wright realized that the bullets in his trunk were for the gun under the front seat. The bullets for the gun that he was holding were actually back at the apartment. His thoughts told him to get the gun from under the front seat, but two gunshots blasting into his open trunk cancelled his thoughts. One bullet lay embedded in the metal while the other bullet entered his right shoulder. "Shit! Uuugh!" he groaned and yelled in agony. "That motherfucka shot me! Ain't this a bitch?" His empty gun fell from his hand as he used his palm to cover the hole in his body. He ducked and ran down the street.

"Write down your mother's address and phone number," Daren commanded Nia. After she did as he ordered, he duct taped her wrists behind her back and took the baby into the bedroom and placed him in the crib. He then went back to the living room, punched Nia in the face, picked up the paper with Nia's mother's information, and neatly folded and tucked it into his pocket. Daren then placed the phone next to where she lay on the floor. "Don't call for ten minutes," he said and he climbed through the window.

Daren quickly pondered if he should go in the direction where Nia told him that William ran or get in his car and search for William and Officer Wright. Suddenly he heard three gunshots off in the distance and he ran in their direction, which was the opposite from where William ran. Instead of running down the long block, he began running through the nearest alley. Hearing footsteps, Daren stooped in the darkness to avoid being seen while he focused on who was approaching. He noticed a man quickly jump and hide behind a parked car.

William was half of a block behind his wounded target and he knew he had but one bullet left. He tried his best to catch up with Officer Wright, but the target that seemed to be slowing down suddenly disappeared. William looked to his left and saw nothing in the dark alley. If he had looked down to his right he would have been aware that Officer Wright was but a foot away from him, stooping down behind a car. Instead, William proceeded to run down the street.

Officer Wright was about to attack William and attempt to take his gun. He knew it would be hard to do with only one arm, but he would try it to save his life. However, William ran off and Officer Wright made sure that he was a good distance down the street before he tiptoed from behind the car and across the sidewalk. He began running up the alley towards the apartment to get another gun to cancel William's life. He could picture shooting William between the eyes.

Once Daren knew that it was Officer Wright approaching, his heart raced even more. Now approximately 20 feet away, Daren stood and stepped out of the darkness. With his left hand, he reached over his face and pulled the ski mask from his chin up to his brow. Simultaneously with his right hand, he pulled the gun up and pointed it at Officer Wright.

Officer Wright stopped in his tracks as if he was looking at a ghost. He then began to smile. "So you're in on this, too? I knew William wasn't smart enough to catch up with me, but I -"

"You had no clue," Daren finished the sentence for him.

"You're right, I had no clue. So you're the brains behind this shit and he's the muscle?"

"I'm the brains and the muscle." Daren's heart began slowing down and he felt calmer.

"Brains and muscle, huh? I can use a man like you on my team. Listen, I apologize for all of that drama I was putting you through. I realized last night that I was wrong for that shit." As his sentence concluded, Daren cocked back the hammer to his gun. Officer Wright's heart began to beat faster and he began experiencing shortness of breath. His eyes also widened at the site he was beholding. He never faced the barrel of a loaded gun before.

"Look, Daren, don't do this. You have a nice job and a good future ahead of you. Look, just hand me the gun and let me take care of William. You and I can work out some things later." He paused and noticed that Daren was looking at him like he was crazy. "Okay, okay! You shoot William, but you and I can still work this out. I won't bother or harass you anymore. I got lots of money. Daren, don't do this shit," and with those pleading words, Officer Wright dropped to his knees. He began believing that Daren wouldn't budge and his life flashed before him.

At the same time, Daren's mind began racing. He thought of how Officer Wright tortured the men in the paddy wagon, about the harassing phone calls, the threats on his life, the pictures he gave to Raquel, and how he overall tried to control his life. He knew it would be hard to deal with his conscience after taking another man's life. A few of his relatives and plenty of his friends have shared their experiences of murder with him. He knew of the dreams, the nightmares, paranoia, and the guilt that came with murdering someone. He *uncocked* the gun.

"Daren, I'm bleeding. Take me to the hospital, man." He sensed Daren was softening.

Daren looked into Officer Wright's happy eyes. Suddenly his mind jumped to the other night when he and Shar-baby were in the park and Officer Wright threatened to kill him. He then cocked the hammer again and aimed.

"Daren, no!"

The last site Officer Wright saw was the flash of light from Daren's gun. His frightened expression gave his face a petrified, horrific look as he fell backward on the alley's broken cement. The tiny hole in his forehead began to trickle a small stream of blood. It appeared that he was looking at the sky as a river of blood began to pour from the huge hole in the rear of his head.

"Blue," a voice whispered from a distance. Daren looked up and noticed William coming up the alley. "Let's roll." They both threw their weapons near the pile of trash. A second later they heard police sirens. "Blue, we gotta get the fuck out of this area. They comin' for us."

"Chill, Black, they're headed for the apartment," Daren said calmly, but inside he was nervous. The only outward evidence of this was his hands, which continued to shake. Nevertheless, they patiently walked in the direction where William thought Officer Wright had run while he was hiding behind the car. After getting to the end of the block they put their masks in their pockets and ran to Daren's car. Less than a minute later they were headed east on Sheriff Road and were back in PG County.

CHAPTER 26

It's been two days and I feel so relaxed. Now that Officer Wright is out of the way, the lives of many people will be much better off, including mine. His life was taken in self-defense; it was either him or me. I think that I've prayed enough on that matter. There goes my phone ringing.

"Hello?"

"Daren, where are you? This is Marcy."

"I'm at the park relaxin'. What's up?"

"Have you read The Washington Post today?" she asks in an anxious voice.

"No," I answer while folding my copy of The Washington Post. I don't want her to know that I know about her husband being killed.

"Okay, listen as I read this to you...."

As she reads the tiny article, I begin to come to grips with the realization that William and I are in the clear. The article says that Anthony Wright was discharged from the police force over two years ago because of illegal drug activity and corruption. He would never report the guns and drugs from his drug busts; he would stash them and then sell everything on the black market. Once he was discharged from the force, he began acting as if he was an undercover policeman and continued "arresting" people and "confiscating" guns and drugs and making big money.

"Ain't that something, Daren? He was killed in a drug deal gone bad. I told him to stop hanging around those streets."

"Are you serious? He was killed? How do you feel? Are you okay?"

"I'm happy. I lost all feeling for him when he put that gun to my head. Actually, I wished he was dead on the night that he threatened my life. You know what else?"

"What?"

"I have two insurance policies on him. Do you need some money?"

Sweetie, I kind of had an insurance policy on your husband, too. "No, you keep your money."

"Daren, I retired from work this morning. I already told my boss to kiss my ass."

"You have that much money coming to you?" I ask in a surprised tone.

"Yes, and I'm going to spend some on you because I know he put you through a lot. Plus, you didn't sell me out and the average person making your salary would have. So tell me what you want."

As I ponder on an answer to appease
Marcy, I notice Nia pull up in her car. "Marcy,
I'll think of something later on. I have to
run."

"You and I can take a cruise somewhere
or you can get rid of that old economy car
and get a real one."

"Okay, sweetie. Let me think about it
and call you back." As I hang up I feel cold
metal on the left side of my head.

"You're going to pay for punching me in
my face," Nia says with anger. "Step your ass
out of the car." The next thing I hear is a loud
ringing in my ear. Nia then backs away laughing with her cell phone in hand.

"You thought I was scared?" I ask.

"Don't even try it! You were shook!"
she says laughing.

"Shook? I was about to shake your ass."

"I'm sorry, baby," she says while forc-
ing a hug on me. "My sister would be upset if
you hurt me. She's getting out of jail soon."

"For real? How much was her bail?"

"Nothing. Since the first officer on the
scene wasn't really an officer, they had no
choice but to drop the charges. We may even
sue."

"Mo' money, mo' money, mo money!"
we say in unison and laugh.

"It ain't like I ain't paid already. Thank
you for keeping your word, Daren."

"That's all a man has," I say giving her
a serious look.

"Does this man have a girlfriend?"

"Yes," I say lying.

"Do you abuse her like you abused me?"

"I didn't abuse you, I only -"

"Bullshit, Daren! I told you, 'Don't hit me too hard!' What did you do? You hit me like I was a damn man. You ain't Mike Tyson, sucka!"

"You told me to hit you to make things look more realistic. If I would have hit you softly, it wouldn't have looked real."

"I know. I'm just messing with you because I'm in a good mood."

"How is your face?"

"Oh, it's alright. It really didn't hurt because you hit like a bitch." Nia then busts out laughing. "No, that shit did hurt on the real. I swear I was knocked out for a minute or two because I don't remember you leaving the apartment."

"For real? You don't remember me telling you to wait ten minutes before calling the police?"

"All I remember is waking up and seeing stars 'n shit. Then I started dialing the police with my tongue."

"With your tongue?"

"Uh huh. It was awkward, but I did it."

"So you're straight?"

"I will be in a minute. Where's that thing you got for me?" she asks referring to her share of the kilos of cocaine. The three of us got a couple pounds of weed, eight kilos of cocaine, and approximately $160,000 each.

Well, I don't want anything to do with any cocaine so I sold four of my kilos to William for $60,000 and the other four to Nia at the same price. They are going to get around $100,000 after selling them, but I don't care. I'll take the $60,000 and not feel paranoid. Just give me the cash.

"That thing is over there by those bushes," I say pointing.

"Good! I'm going to break them things down and get paid!"

"That's what Black said."

"As long as he don't sell them on me and my sister's territory it's all good." Nia pauses and then looks over to me. "You know that you can call me whenever you need something, right?"

"Okay."

"I mean anything."

"Okay. I will."

"Give me a hug."

I squeeze her tightly and she kisses my cheek.

"Thanks again, Daren."

I decide to take the long way home to be sure that I'm not being followed. While driving I'm blasting my music and yelling in celebration of having some *real money*. I ain't used to having a damn thing and now I'm holding almost $300,000. I'm happy as I don't know what!

I'm sitting here mentally spending every dime of it. After calming down a little and driving over ten miles I realize that I'm not being tailed. I drop some of the money at my grandmother's, some at my mother's, some in my bank account, and the rest at my home. I tuck $3,000 in my pocket and head to Pentagon City to get some clothes and some CDs. You know what? I don't even have a DVD player yet. I should buy one of those...maybe I should buy two.

It feels good to know that I can have anything that I want. Walking with several bags and tons of confidence, I stop at Karibu to pick up a couple of books. As I browse the shelves I notice a kind pair of eyes on a beautiful woman that looks like she's hurting inside.

"Hello, sweetie. I don't profess to know your business, but whatever it is that's on your mind, you're more than welcome to tell me about it."

She looks at me in shock. Damn, she is so pretty, but her beauty is of elegance, which makes her stand apart from the average woman. She's the type that you'd buy a fancy dress and take to a black-tie affair. Wherever you take her or whatever you buy her, it has to be classy.

"I'm Daren. Let's go down to the food court and talk about what's on your mind. What's your name, sweetie?"

"I'm Libra. It's nice to meet you, Daren. Sure, we can talk. How can you tell I have some serious things on my mind?"

"Libra, it's written all over your face."

CHAPTER 27

Butter stood in the mirror getting her face and thoughts together. Robin had convinced her to go with her to Virginia Beach for some fresh air and to clear her mind. The drama within Butter's marriage had gotten worse, and Robin always made attempts to help ease the pain and the stress. Every now and then Butter went with her to the hairdresser and the spa, but since Donald began spending more time away from home, she would decline Robin's invitations and stay at home. She had originally declined her invite for a weekend at the beach even after Robin told her she'd pay for everything.

However, all of that changed when she got a visit from William. She had already lifted the restraining order on him and, behind her husband's back, began granting him visitation with Billy. He actually saw Billy a couple of times during the week and would be getting him for the entire weekend.

The big surprise came two days ago when William handed her fifty $100 bills. Butter damn-near pissed on herself after counting it. She even rubbed it with her fingers, held it up to the light, and wet a bill or two just to see if the money was real or counterfeit. She couldn't believe that William had given her money, not to mention the fact that it was such a large amount. In all reality, Butter had never held that much money in her hand.

Money had become tight since Donald began bringing home less from his paycheck, and she could use the $5,000 that William gave her. On top of that, William said he'd be giving her more for Billy and some for her to take herself shopping. She wanted to ask questions, but decided against it. As long as the money was real and "spendable," she didn't care where it came from. All that she knew was that she had bills to pay and William's black ass hadn't paid child support consistently since their son was born.

And did she bother to tell her husband about the money? Hell no! Donald would find a reason to spend it on his truck or to buy shoes, jerseys, and video games until every cent disappeared. She played *this one* smart and got a new bank account that only she had access to. She now knew that it was time for her to take control since her husband was acting irresponsibly.

"You ready to have some fun?" Robin asks with a smile as Butter opens the car door.

"Shoot, where the party at!" Butter replies while placing her bags in the back seat. She then sits in the front. "Alright, let's get away from here. I'm ready to drink a little, dance a lot, and wear my two-piece. I don't give a damn if I don't look the way that I want to in it. I might have a gut, but I'm not going to let it stop me. I'm about to start living and having some fun."

"Alright, girl!" Robin says with amazement at Butter's zest. "Let's get you to the beach. I haven't heard you this pumped since before you got married." Robin hits the gas and heads for 495. "So finish telling me what you were saying about William. You aren't thinking about getting back with him, are you?"

"No way! Never that! Girl, don't make me slap you up in here." Both women laugh.

"I'm saying, you made it seem like he was on your good side."

"He gave me $5,000 and said he was giving me more for Billy and some for me."

"Well, you ain't gotta get back with him...but giving him a little pussy won't hurt."

"What?!"

"Tammy, I'm just playing, girl. I don't know why you got involved with him in the first place. The only thing he ever did was help you make that pretty little boy."

"And give me $5,000."

"Okaaay!" They both laugh and Robin changes the subject. "So where's Donald?"

"Your guess is as good as mine. I haven't seen him since he left this morning."

"He knew you were leaving, didn't he?"

"And? He don't care. That's obvious to me now. I've been trying to make things work, but -"

"Marriage ain't what you thought it would be, is it?"

"Nope," Butter quickly responded with her eyes looking straight ahead.

Suddenly Robin's car begins to make noise and then starts to jerk."

"Oh, shit! I think I got a flat tire."

"Do you have a spare in the trunk?" Butter asks.

"Yeah. Can you fix it?"

"I ain't never fixed a flat before, but I'm sure we can fix it together."

Robin and Butter go to the trunk and begin taking out Robin's bags and putting them in the backseat to gain access to the spare tire. They then begin lifting it out of the trunk.

"It won't move," Butter says.

"Girl, you ain't lifting it. Grab it from the bottom."

"I am. It ain't moving. What's that?"

"What?"

"That," Butter said pointing to the center of the rim. "It's screwed down."

"Oh, that's why it ain't moving," Robin says smiling, and she begins to unscrew it.

"You got the tire screwed down and got the nerve to say I ain't lifting," Butter joked sarcastically. "Let me call Donald."

"Shit! Shit! Shit! Shit!" Robin exclaimed loudly while holding her hand up to her face.

"What?"

"I done broke a damn nail! Shit! I just had them done, too."

"You can get it fixed in Virginia."

"I don't know how they are down there. Plus, I only let sistas do my nails. I don't mess with them Asians."

"Don't look at me. I don't mess with them either."

For the next 20 minutes they struggled to unscrew the tire, take it out, and learn how to work the jack without breaking any more nails and getting too dirty. Reading the directions for working the jack was another story all together, and it took even more time. After another 20 minutes they were tired and saw their efforts as a waste. The summer heat was wearing them down, the mosquitoes were biting, the passing cars were scary, and the darkness from the trees on 495 was lurking. Robin and Butter felt uncomfortable.

"Girl, it don't look right out here. I'm about to go sit in the car."

"Me, too," Butter said. "We gotta call somebody to help us."

"What did your husband say?"

"I just left another message on his voicemail. I didn't get an answer and I called him about five times."

"I don't know who to call because I ain't got no man, and all of my old boyfriends are either with a new woman, married, or got an attitude over some dumb stuff. And I was ready to party, too."

"Well, what are we going to do?"

"I don't know what to do. Oooh, I know who to call – Daren."

Fifteen minutes later Robin stood with her arms crossed while Daren blasted her ears with laughter.

"Sweetie, you ain't never changed a tire before? I'm glad I wasn't far away. You need to learn how to do these things on your own."

Robin tried to frown, but she found herself smiling. "Well, that's why I have this strong, handsome man to my rescue. Do your thing, Daren."

"Just call me Superman, baby," Daren smiled as he jacked the car up higher. "This jack is broken or something. Why is it so hard to jack it up? Wait, I'm going to get the jack from my car."

"Oh, that ain't the problem," Robin smiles. "Tammy, get out of the car! Daren's trying to jack it up!"

Daren looks at Butter getting out of the car with a weird expression. "Oh, I know damn well you ain't sittin' in there while I'm tryin' to change this tire. Y'all done lost y'all's minds. Y'all are crazy. What's up, Tamela? Why are you so quiet? You knew I was out here and you didn't want to come speak? How is your son doing?"

Butter was staring at Daren as he fixed the tire and chatted with Robin. She just looked on and reminisced about back when they were together.

"Tamela?"

"Oh, he's fine. The teacher said he's improving and he's going to pass. I think he needs glasses."

"He got his eyes from his mother."

"So what are you saying, Daren?"

"Anyway," Daren says as he takes his eyes from Butter and places them on Robin, "y'all should stay in town tonight, get the tire fixed first thing in the morning, and then leave out."

"What's wrong with this one? We can't make it down there with this one?"

"It's a spare and it's only good for temporary use, not for driving three hours to Virginia Beach. And if one of these other tires goes flat what are you going to use then? You're already using your spare."

"Oh, okay. I feel you," Robin says. "What'cha say, girl? You cool?"

"I guess we leave in the morning. We're already over an hour behind."

"Good," Daren looked on. "Now go put some air in that spare because it's looking a little flat. I'll see y'all later."

"What?" Robin asked confused. "Are you done?"

"Oh, y'all straight."

"Damn that was fast! It was only five minutes. Thank you for coming through for us."

"It's never a problem for my girls," Daren says as he gives Robin a huge hug and gives Butter a shoulder hug. He leans forward and pats her on the back as their chests barely touch.

As the two women walk back to the car, Butter can't wait to talk. "Umph! Girl, I got so wet watching him change that tire. I ain't even going to lie. His arms were looking good! I just feel so good when he's around me," Butter went on blushing and talking about Daren.

"Uh huh, you think you slick, don't you?"

"What, Robin?"

"You were putting on your make-up when he got here. That's why you were busy in the car when he was trying to jack it up."

"You know it! Had to look my best."

"That's how you should want things for your husband."

"Now why did you have to bring him up? You messed up my mental flow just now."

"I'm sorry. It's just that I think you married the wrong man. Daren's the man for you."

"I don't want to hear it. I really don't. Let me out."

Robin laughed as she came to a stop. "I'll call you real early in the morning to pick you up."

"I'll be ready."

Butter goes into her dark apartment and realizes that Donald had been there and had left. She hadn't seen him since that morning, and he couldn't even come home to say goodbye to her, but as soon as she leaves he comes there and leaves back out. Butter was also upset that he never returned her calls when she and Robin were stranded, and was even more upset that he didn't answer it upon seeing her number come up on the caller I.D. She knew it was on because it rang several times. If it was off the voicemail would have come on automatically.

Butter was cleaning up the kids' room when the tears of hurt and disappointment began to flow. She fell to her knees and clasped her hands together.

"Dear Lord, please bless me with the knowledge and wisdom to make better life decisions. I love You and I'm grateful that You've blessed me with a handsome son, a good job, and a healthy body. I just want to know if my marriage is worth holding on to. I've been trying my best to love him and to be patient, but I'm hurting inside. I'm not happy and I'm feeling depressed. Please, Lord, if this marriage isn't meant to be, please show me a sign. I just ask that You make me a stronger woman and a better person since

I've endured so much. Thank you, Jesus. I don't want to hurt anymore. I just pray this pain would go away. And thank you for the $5,000 and for letting me and Billy's father get along better, but please don't put us back together -"

Her prayer is interrupted by her cell phone.

"Hello?"

"Tamela, what's up?" Donald asks. "How's your trip? You and Robin at the beach already?"

Butter hesitated to respond in hopes of gaining insight on Donald's whereabouts. "Yes, we're about to check-in. Where are you?"

"Oh, I'm at home. Yeah, just sittin' down here watching TV and about to order a pizza."

Butter stood to her feet and walked into the living room where Donald claimed to have been. There was no Donald in the living room. She then closed her eyes at the sound of his lies. *Thank you, Jesus, for showing me a sign.*

*

I haven't seen Butter since her wedding day, but she's still looking good. I can tell that she's not happy, but at least she's taking care of herself. I guess dealing with that husband of hers is taking a toll on her. Damn, I know her so well and I could see in her eyes that she had a lot to say to me. But, hey, let her husband and Robin deal with all of that. It's really her personal business and I ain't getting involved.

And her and Robin almost spoiled my groove tonight. I will be hooking up with Libra in a few minutes. I've talked to her a couple of times since we met at Karibu earlier this week. I sure don't want to be late for our first time getting together. Okay, let me see...8452..yup, there's her condo.

"Hey, beautiful lady," I say as I step through the door while looking her in her eyes. This woman is too beautiful and if she acts right she will be the lucky woman to be called my wife. "Where's your bathroom? I need to wash my hands." I follow her directions and return to the living room and give her a big hug. "Libra, you are looking nice tonight."

"Thank you. What do you want to do? Mmmm, this is a nice hug. You hungry? Would you like to watch a movie?"

"Baby, I want to sit down here and talk to your soul. I want to learn about you and your world. If you can handle my being honest, I want to share myself with you. I want to tell you my life and what brought me here."

We chat briefly and Libra gets up to get some strawberries and champagne. I go to help her and as she washes the strawberries, I rinse them and place them on the tray. We continue to talk and we're actually clicking pretty well. She is very funny and being around her is cool. As we finish washing the strawberries we return to the blanket on the living room floor, me carrying the tray and she with the bottle of Asti. We continue talking for an hour without touching the strawberries or drinking the champagne. She's in the Internet Technology field, makes $85,000 a year, no kids, was married once for three years, and her ex-husband physically and emotionally abused her. She wants to lose ten pounds, wants to get married within two years, wants two kids, and a new job that makes six figures. Damn, I just love listening to a woman talk.

"Libra, we ain't touch these strawberries yet and the champagne is warm," I say as I stand. "I'm going to put the champagne back in the frigerator."

"I'll do it, baby. You relax. I'll get it."

"Relax, cutie. I got you. Plus, I'm already standing."

"Okay, baby. Just grab a bottle of Dom."

"We already opened the Asti."

"Okay, baby. We'll drink the Asti later. It's just champagne. Who cares?"

Just champagne? I damn sure can't afford Dom. Wait a minute, I'm paid now. I can afford some Dom and some Cristal if I want it. I return to her and pop the bottle.

"Cutie, eat one of those strawberries so I can se them touch those sexy lips." Without hesitating she slowly holds a strawberry to her lips and bites through it revealing bright, white, straight teeth. I pick up three fat strawberries and drop them in my glass of Dom. I then pick up a fourth strawberry from the tray and bite into it. As we sip, chew, and smile, I take the initiative and pick a strawberry for her with my right hand, place it over her left shoulder, and bring it around her neck to her right shoulder. I then feed it to her and as she bites I instinctively bite the other half.

As our lips connect with the strawberry, they connect with each other. We both begin to kiss comfortably and slowly with the strawberry pieces in our mouths. However, we share the pieces while almost ignoring them due to our tongues dancing together. We begin learning how the other's tongue works, and I reach into the glass of Dom and retrieve a soaked strawberry. I then hold it to our lips and we taste it as we kiss and the passion gets deeper. I then place my Dom drenched fingers in her mouth and she sucks them while kissing me and eating the strawberry. I haven't had so much fun with champagne since Butter -, c'mon Daren, don't think about her. Anyway, I concentrate on Libra because she has some skills with her tongue and, if everything goes as planned, one day that'll be my "longberry" being soothed, licked, and sucked like she's doing those strawberries.

We continue kissing, finger licking, and strawberry slushing, and I begin letting the Dom drop from the strawberries onto her neck and then licking it off. This must be her spot because she's moaning.

"Daren...wait."

Hey, I'm just kissing and enjoying her comfort, so if she wants to stop then cool. "Wait? Okay, cutie. What's up? What do you want to do, talk?"

"No. We've done enough of that. Just keep kissing me and follow me." Libra grabs my hand and leads me to her bedroom. On the way there I continue kissing, squeezing, and touching, and once there, she draws open the curtains to the balcony to reveal the view overlooking hills and other condos. She then slowly undresses while looking at me seductively. "Make love to me, Daren."

I surely didn't expect this to happen so soon. I undress almost as slowly as she does, and as I lay down she puts my longberry into her warm mouth and begins to massage it with loving precision. "This feels so good, Libra." My mind drifts away as the sucking continues. Between slurps I hear Libra ask me to make love to her so I reach into my pocket, rip open the box of condoms, and grab one without stopping her from her oral fixation. I never plan on having sex, but I keep condoms on me just in case.

Once I rip the condom wrapper open, Libra lay down and, even with a condom on, I can feel the friction of her walls squeezing my longberry. I begin to make love to her body very slowly. Her breasts are small and firm and her skin is soft. She has a small pouch, but who gives a damn? A real woman is a real woman and I'm enjoying every inch of her. She is moaning with delight and we are beginning to connect emotionally. We lock our hands together in one tight grip and I place them above her head on the bed. All that I can feel are her hands, her tight vaginal walls, and her soft, pretty legs wrapped around my lower back. This love making is sweet, and I lower my lips to her neck and begin tonguing again. I keep our hands above her head as my tongue goes back and forth from her neck to her tongue. We have so much to give each other and I'm really in need of her form of love. Oh yes! I'm about to come.

"Are you about to come, baby?"

Now how did she know that? Is she an angel? "Yes, baby."

Libra immediately sits up. "Take your condom off, baby." As I do so she begins sucking me with wild ferocity. I lost my stroke and concentration when I pulled out so my orgasm has been delayed. Libra then turns around on her hands and knees, backs that ass up, and places me in her without a condom. After several pumps she turns around and sucks my longberry for a minute, then she turns back around and puts me back inside her wet vagina. She goes back and forth with the "all around the world" fuck and suck technique until I begin to come again. As my juice begins to shoot like a rocket, she places me into her mouth and sucks extra hard. This extra pressure makes me go crazy and I just know I'm in heaven.

"Oh! Baby, baby, you can stop now."

"Okay, baby. Let me know if you want more, okay?" she asks as I pull her to cuddle next to me and begin stroking her short hairdo. She can talk after I came in her mouth? That means she swallowed! Yes, I ain't letting her go anywhere. I lucked up this time.

*

Butter wakes up from her position on the floor next to her son's bed. She can't believe that after praying she cried herself to sleep. She gets up to see what time it is on the microwave in the kitchen and she hears odd sounds from her bedroom. Butter's heart begins to beat rapidly and she experiences a slight shortness of breath. *I'm going to stab her and him,* she thinks to herself. She grabs a knife and softly walks to her bedroom and braces herself for the woman Donald is fucking in her bed. She peeks in and nothing could have braced her for the shock of what her eyes see. Her husband Donald is having sex and hitting the ass from the back – but it is the asshole of a man. At the same time there is another man with himself inside of Donald from the back. All three of the men are hunched over.

Butter looks on breathlessly as she digests the scene. *I just woke up so I must be dreaming,* she thinks to herself, but as the man that Donald is fucking begins to grunt and scream, Butter realizes that this is indeed a reality. Her heart begins to feel like it will pop out of her chest at any second. She noticed that no one in the bed had a condom on and the air was laced with pure funk.

"You nasty motherfucker..." Butter hears herself whisper. The three, not hearing her, continue stroking and grunting and Butter suddenly feels her breath come back. "You nasty motherfuckers!"

The three men look up and stop the ménage trois. Donald looks on in a happy daze. "Basil, take your dick out of me," he says.

Butter doesn't shed a tear, but she runs for the door. "I don't believe the shit I saw and the shit I smell!"

Donald follows her out of the apartment into the foyer area down one level of stairs. "Come back. Tamela, let me explain. Come on back and meet my friends." Watching his wife leave the building, he walks upstairs to his apartment. While chewing his cheek he gets back in bed with Basil and Trey.

Butter begins driving and immediately calls William. "Hey, I need you to watch Billy for a week or two," she says in a demanding tone, one that was ready for verbal backlash. To her surprise, William says, "Okay, no problem. I got another $5,000 for you, too." She couldn't believe her ears, and she felt that God was working with her because William is normally extremely hard to get along with. *Wait a minute, he agrees to keep our child for two weeks and he just gave me $5,000 and tells me he has another $5,000 for me? This is a baby mother's dream.*

After calmly talking with William for another minute she calls Robin to let her know she's on her way.

"Girl, what's wrong?"

"Nothing. I just can't sleep and I don't want to be home alone. Plus, it would be easier for us to leave in the morning straight from your house."

Butter slept like a baby at Robin's house and never once did she shed a tear over the horrific scene of her husband sleeping with two men.

CHAPTER 28

Me and Libra have been fucking like jackrabbits. It's been a month now and we go out to fancy dinners with $50 entrees, and we ring up $200 dinner bills. We take long strolls through malls, parks, and we drive up to Baltimore Harbor, walk the piers, and talk for hours. We even got tickets for the Erykah Badu concert that takes place in a couple of days. We also shower together, prepare meals together, watch movies together, and turn around and talk some more. By the end of the night we're fucking again, but that's cool because that's not all that we do.

Last Sunday I made plans to cook us a nice, romantic dinner. Libra likes to sing at karaoke so since she would be performing that night at 6 PM, we agreed on having dinner at 9 PM. That would give her ample time to get *her sing* on, entertain the crowd, and get home. What did she do? She called at

8:30 and said she was still at the event. Next thing I knew, it began to thunderstorm and she called back at 10 PM saying she had to drive her friend home because the woman's husband left her and refused to pick her up. Now that was cool as long as she got home safely. I didn't have a problem with any of that and I'm not mad that she missed dinner because things come up sometimes. Plus, I know how it is to be involved with something you really love; sometimes you can lose track of time and forget what other plans you made. My main concern was that she got home safely in that nasty thunderstorm.

The problem came upon her arrival home, which was at about 11:30 PM. She apologized all night and all of the next three days. All of that wasn't called for because I understood the situation, and I wasn't even sweatin' the issue or acting mad. She really got on my nerves because she would bring it up several times a day, "Oh, Daren, I am so sorry. Are you mad at me? I'll make it up to you." I got tired of hearing that.

But I'm good at adapting to situations. It was too late to eat that night so I ran her a hot, steamy, bubble bath with violets in the water. It was so sexy and she was amazed at the beauty of the room. I took my time and put together a nice atmosphere.

Not only that, I paid close attention to her when we were at the mall a few days before. I was checking on some basketball jerseys while she browsed the jewelry store across from the store I was in. When she went to the next store to look at some shoes, I ran to the jewelry store and bought the ring that she was looking at without telling her. While she was in the tub enjoying my company, and me feeding her the dinner that I cooked like she was a baby, she looked up and noticed the case in the soap dish.

"What's that?" Libra asked.

"I don't know. You tell me."

She looked at me and her confused face transformed into all teeth and bright eyes. She grabbed the case and opened it and her jaw dropped open.

"Oh, baby! How did you know? Oh, you are so wonderful! I can't believe you! I really like this ring and I was about to get it!"

Yes, she was hooked that night and has been ever since. The next day when I came over she had a wardrobe of underwear, socks, a pair of pants, and about five shirts for me. Surprisingly all of them fit. One good thing about women buying underwear, they buy what they picture a man in, and they picture a man in what turns them on. If a man wants to know what turns a woman on, he simply needs to ask that woman. Anyway, I'm surprised at my baby's taste because I will actually wear these shirts in public. This classy woman can dress me anytime.

We are supposed to go work out at the gym tonight at 10 PM, but it's now 11 PM and

I've seen no sign of her. She sings almost every other night and, since singing is her true love, I don't interfere. I even went to watch and support her a few nights back and she did pretty good. I was thoroughly impressed with her vocal skills. She sung Whitney Houston's "I'll Always Love You" and she was so happy that I was there. We listened to others sing, shot some pool, then went back to her place where she apologized for standing me up last Sunday some more. The good part came when she oral sexually thanked me for watching her sing and clapping louder than anyone else. Now, the head she gave me that night was supreme. But, anyway, she's standing me up again tonight so I'm just going to work out alone and talk to her in the morning.

***

Butter sat across from Richard and tried to appear as if she was having a good time. The food was good, the music was just right, and he could work his body on the dance floor. Butter also like Richard's body. He had everything going for him, but he kept saying the wrong things. *If only he would shut his mouth he may get some,* she thought. It's been a long time since she made love, and she wanted someone to "validate" her attractiveness and "erase" the thoughts of her making love to a husband that made love to men.

"Tamela, you got some pretty toes," Richard says as he looks under the restaurant table. "Girl, I'll suck your toes and some more stuff. I got plenty of skills. Watch this."

Butter stared in horror as Richard opened his mouth and made his tongue move like a wave.

"Did you like that? I know you did? So what kind of men do you like?"

"Quiet ones," Butter said with agitation in her voice. She was about done with his mouth and the entire date.

Richard didn't notice Butter's mood. "Quiet? I like to make noise when I do it to you. You seem quiet yourself, but I'd have you making noises. I'd have you calling my name like 'Richard! Oh, Richard!'"

Butter looked at him like he was crazy.

"Tamela, I'm just playing with you...but I can do it good."

"Oops! Look at the time," Butter said as she stood from the table and placed the napkin on her plate. "I have to pick my son up."

"Pick your son up? You got a son?"

"Yes."

"Good! He can keep my kids company. I have four of them –three girls and one boy."

"That's nice," Butter says while sliding her pocketbook over her shoulder.

"Look, let's pick up your son and take him to stay with my son and daughter while you and I –"

"I thought you said you had three daughters?"

"That's with my other babies' mothers. Me and my first one had two kids together. The second two only had one daughter each. We can take your son to my first babies' mother's house because she never minds watching other people's kids."

Motherfucka, you just totally lost all cool points in my book. I will never...ever mess with you, kiss you, sex you, or go out with you again. I won't even let you kiss my pretty toes. "Richard, the mother of your first two children sounds like a really nice woman, but I'll have to pass on the invitation. I'm a little too tired, and I don't know her to be leaving my son with her."

"Why don't we...let's just...okay..., what time does your son have to be picked up? Because we can go back to my place real quick, or if it's too far and you have to pick up your son real soon, then we can hit a motel."

"No! You done stuck your dick in enough pussy and you need to be in the presence of the small tribe that you've created. You got four kids by three different women, and you're still running around thinking you're a player, bragging on how good your sex is, and trying to get more women in the bed. You disgust me! Don't make me say some shit that I don't want to say. Just take me home, please. As a matter of fact, I'll get a ride. Take care of yourself and be a man. Bye! And don't ever call me."

Richard looks at Butter with great surprise. "Who you talking to. You don't even know me, bitch. Fuck you."

Butter doesn't bother to entertain his words. She just strolls out of the restaurant and hails the first cab that comes. As she reaches for the door she says, "I ain't never dating or getting married again."

***

It's now 12:45 the next afternoon and I'm cutting my grandmother's grass. When I finish I'm going to cut her hair and...let me stop this lawnmower and answer this call. "Hello?"

"Daren, I need you. I'm so sick right now."

It's Libra. "Sick? What happened?"

"They kept buying me margaritas and I drank too many."

"How many is *too* many?"

"Seven. I threw up in my car, on the driver side door outside of my car, and I've been throwing up all morning. I need you to come take care of me."

"You got the runs, too, don't you?"

"Daren!"

"Diarrhea, you got diarrhea?"

"Yes."

"And you expect me to come over there?" I ask jokingly.

"C'mon, Daren. I need you."

"Okay, I'll come over if I can. I'm busy doing yard work and I have a few other things to do afterwards. If I finish early enough I'll be over there; if not, I'll see you tomorrow for the concert."

I know that she doesn't expect for me to have sympathy for a hangover? She done lost her mind. So she stood me up for her alcohol buddies and her alcohol addiction? Sike, but the fact remains that it's only a hangover - if she *hangs* in there she'll get *over* it.

CHAPTER 29

In the past, Butter wouldn't have dreamed of keeping Donald waiting for her. She was a stickler when it came to time and she believed in being punctual at all costs. However, she walked into Jasper's with a stride not to be denied by anyone. It was full of confidence and exuberance and sure to let others know that she wasn't to be played with. Her business suit was on point and appeared to have been designed for her exclusively. Circumstances beyond her control had forced the creation of a *new her* and it was a person that she loved.

Donald had been waiting for almost 20 minutes. Normally he would chew Butter out, but this particular day and time the shoe was on the other foot. Power between the two of them had shifted from him to her, and he came to that humbling realization days before. He hadn't spoken to his wife but for the brief conversation to arrange their meeting. He really didn't know what to expect.

"How are you doing, Tamela?" he asked just to break the ice.

"I'm doing fine. And you?"

"I'm alright."

"Good...good," Butter said while staring directly into his eyes and enjoying how weak he had become. "And how is your asshole?"

"Why you gotta say some foul shit like that? We are supposed to be talking like adults and -"

"And what?" Butter said while holding her position ready for battle.

"Okay, look, let's start all over without any conflict, please."

Butter felt that his backing down was victory enough for her. "Okay. I just wanted you to sign these papers here for the divorce...hold on a second." She quickly shuffled through her manila folder. "Here they are...just sign next to all of the X's."

"So you want a divorce?"

"Look at the top of that paper - *Divorce Decree*. Can you see that?"

"I see it." Donald put his head down and began signing each document. Without looking up he says, "So what happened that night?"

"You don't know? You were there."

"I kind of know, but I don't know exactly what happened. I remember bits and pieces. What did you see?"

"I saw you and two other men having sex and y'all were -"

"Okay. That's enough. I'm sorry you had to see that."

"Why? Were you gay all along?"

"I'm not gay."

"You're not gay?"

"No, I'm not."

"Okay. Well...how do I word this...how long have you been having sex with men?"

"That's not really how it happened," Donald pleaded.

"How did it happen? I'm listening."

"I was taking ecstasy and you really can't control your hormones when you're on it. One time me and some friends took it together and we had sex."

"All of y'all together? All men?"

"Two men and one woman. I started taking Viagra to stay hard because ecstasy stops your erection."

"Did all of this happen before or after we got married?"

"Right before we got married."

"Did you sign all of those documents? You missed an X on that one. Sign right there."

"Right here?"

"Yes, right there." Butter began thinking to herself and decided to keep going with her thoughts. "Donald, did you happen to have sex on the couch in the living room or on any other piece of furniture in our apartment?"

"No, just our bedroom."

"Our bedroom? That's yours! I wouldn't sleep in that bed if Morris Chestnut, Shemar Moore, and Tyrese were in it waiting on me. The thought of those three men sound good to you, don't it?"

Donald wanted to say something mean in response, but he elected to ignore her.

"Anyway, you can have the bed."

"I don't want it."

"Donald, what do you want?"

"Just my clothes. You can have everything else. No, I want my TV and my video games, too."

"Okay. I'm coming to get everything else. I'll talk to you later." Butter stood from the table and walked out of Jasper's. *I'm going to have me a moving sale and get paid. Then I'm going to take the money and hit the mall,* she smiled.

CHAPTER 30

I ain't seen my cutie-pie in two days and I'm missing her. Today is the big day – the Erykah Badu concert up in Baltimore at Pier 6. I've already called Libra and told her to be ready by 4:30 PM because the show starts at 6 PM and we have a 30-minute drive. We also have to find a place to park; not to mention a 45-minute window for her to be late getting dressed. After all, she is a woman that likes to look good.

I arrive at her condo at 4 PM and she peeks out of the shower.

"Baby, we need to stop at my mother's," she says.

"For what?"

"I left the shoes for my outfit over there."

Here we go. She could have gotten those shoes all morning or afternoon and she's going to wait until two hours before the concert. "Alright. Don't keep Erykah waiting. You know she wants to see us."

"Boy, you are so silly," she laughs.

As she showers I iron my clothes, and the second she jumps out, I jump in. It takes me ten minutes to wash and five minutes to get dressed. I count $500, and I put $200 in my pocket and $300 in the empty canister above her frigerator. It's now 4:45.

"Let's roll, cutie-pie," I say opening the front door.

"Daren, how do I look?"

"Like a queen. Baby, you are gorgeous."

She blushes and we walk down two flights of stairs to my car. "Baby, where are the tickets?"

She fumbles through her purse for a minute. "They're upstairs. I thought I had them. I'll go get them."

"I'll get them," I say and I jump out and dash up the two flights and back down with the tickets. She must be out of her mind if she thought I'd let her go get them. She'd take all day and we'd be super late then.

We get to her mother's at 5:05. She looks through the tiny window in the door and then cracks it.

"Hello, Mrs. Sumter. Your daughter sent me to grab her shoes from the den. She said they're in a box on the floor."

"You got dog doo-doo on your feet?"

"Huh?" What in the hell is she talking about?

"Do you have dog doo-doo on your feet?" Mrs. Sumter asks again.

"No," I respond while quickly holding them up to check for myself.

"Let me see your feet." She opens the door all of the way and checks my shoes. "Okay, you're fine. There was a dog out here earlier and he messed on the grass right over there. Libra's daddy stepped in it and tracked it through the house on my good rug."

What in the hell is going on? I didn't walk anywhere near where she pointed and she took me through all of that. She is too funny. I glance at my watch and get back on topic. "Mrs. Sumter, can you get the shoes, or would you like me to get them?"

"Yes, come on in and get them. Oh, baby, do me a favor. My husband is at the store getting some carpet cleaner and a carpet steamer. Could you go down in the basement and grab the shovel and a trash bag out of the washroom? You're dressed nice. Y'all got somewhere to be?"

"Well, we're running late for the concert and –"

"This won't take long. Aw, bless your heart. I need you to shovel all of that dog mess into a bag for me, hear, baby?"

"Yes."

I can't believe this shit. Mrs. Sumter is walking along the grass like an inspector pointing out dog mess, I'm following behind her with the shovel and picking up whatever she points to, and Libra is in the car embarrassed.

"Momma, we gotta go."

"Girl, hush! We won't be but a second and that concert ain't goin' nowhere. That ol' ugly-looking dog messed my grass all up. He better not let me catch him 'round here!"

I did not want to clean the shovel and put it back in the basement so I put it on the side of the house. I put the bag in the trashcan right next to it and ran in the house to wash my hands. We're back in the car and it's now 5:40. We're definitely going to be late, but what's done is done. Besides, I had to look out for moms because she can cook a slammin' sweet potato pie.

"Daren, I am so sorry and so embarrassed. I can't believe my mother."

"Baby, don't sweat it. We're about to have a lot of fun tonight." With those words I push the tape in and Jay-Z's "Big Pimpin'" blasts through my tiny speakers. As I dance and rap Libra laughs at me. As I continue to do the entire song again and again, she becomes hysterical with laughter. As usual, she and I are having a wonderful time and we haven't even gotten to the event yet. I rewind the song several times until we finally arrive in Baltimore. As we get to the gate we can hear "Love" being performed. "Damn! I didn't know Musiq would be here!"

"I didn't either," Libra says with wide eyes. "He's not mentioned on the ticket."

"C'mon! Let's go catch him."

We find our seats and slow dance to

the rest of his song. Then Musiq tells everyone to stand up and the band starts playing
"Girlfriend." Me and Libra stand up and start
dancing. She dances like a white girl, but it's
alright because she's my baby. I smile, tickle
her, and keep dancing my two-step.

We are having fun and we ain't even
seen Erykah yet. The entire crowd is jammin'.
The band stops, Musiq says his "thank yous"
and "good-byes," and he leaves. The master
of ceremony now grabs the mic. "Ladies and
gentlemen, we are going to take a ten-minute
break and our feature attraction, Ms.Erykah
Badu, will be right out. Ten minutes exactly
so don't go far."

We all sit down and the crowd is still
buzzing from Musiq's performance. I grab the
bottom of my shirt and begin to pump it so
that the air can cool me down. I then sing
the chorus while looking at my cutie-pie, "I
just wanna know your name and maybe
sometime...we can hook up...hang out...just
chill." I can't tell if Libra is laughing because
I'm singing to her or if she's laughing because I can't sing. I put my arm around her
and continue fanning and pumping my shirt.
My watch reads 6:31.

All of a sudden, Libra looks at me with
a blank expression. "So where were you last
night?"

"After all of that yard work and running
all of those errands, I just showered and fell
asleep watching TV."

"Daren, don't fuckin' lie to me! I know you were with a woman. You don't have to lie to me."

I look into her eyes and see a totally different woman than the one I was growing to love in the past month or so. "Cutie, I was alone."

"Bullshit! You were with some woman!"

I try not to laugh or feel disrespected because of her raising her voice. "Cutie –"

"Don't give me that 'cutie' shit! Where were you?"

Now Musiq's audience has transformed into me and Libra's audience. They are now quiet and I can feel that they're looking at us. This woman done made a scene up in here.

"You really need to lower your voice. Not only are you talking in a way that I'm not having, and not only are you looking too pretty to try to look ugly, but you're making a scene. Everyone was talking to each other a minute ago, now they're quiet. Why? Because they're listening to us."

"Fuck who's watching. Daren, I don't give a fuck! I told you that I was sorry for standing you up for dinner and I told you I was sorry for not coming home and working out with you the other day. You had no right to go out with some bitch last night. I had too much to drink and now you're messing around on me and trying to make me pay for it."

"Where do you get this idea from? No-body ain't –"

"I'M FUCKIN' TALKIN'! DON'T INTERUPT ME!"

I keep my voice low and calm and look her in her eyes. "You better act like you got some damn sense...actin' like a damn fool up in here. And I don't know who you're cussin' at and raising your voice at, but I ain't the one for takin' no shit from you or anyone else. I don't give a fuck how good you look, you ain't going to talk to me any ol' way you want. You had ample time to talk to me since last night. We could have discussed this shit last night, this morning, this afternoon at your condo while we got ready, in the car going to your mother's, leaving your mother's, and walking from the car coming here. You were having fun driving up here in the car when I was rappin' and dancin'. You were having fun when Musiq had you dancin' to the last song. Now you wanna start some shit? Just calm down and let's enjoy Erykah. That's your girl, ain't it?"

"Fuck Erykah, fuck this –"

"Lower your voice, Libra."

"Okay, I'm sorry," she says in a lower tone, "but fuck Erykah and fuck this concert. She'll be in DC next weekend. I'll buy you two tickets for that show."

"Two?"

"Yes, one for you and one for your bitch."

I begin to laugh. She got me on that

one. I haven't been with any woman but her since we met. "Libra, there's no one but you in my life. I'm trying to find that special woman and settle down. I don't have time to run games. You're the only one, cutie."

"Then why weren't you with me last night?"

"I chose to be alone."

"I was sick and you knew that."

"Sick? Girl, you had a hangover. The only thing you needed for that was time and a toilet. It wasn't like you had a cold or something."

"So you'd rather be with her than me?"

"There is no *her*, only a *you*."

"I'm done talking. Daren, give me the keys."

"For what?"

"My purse is in your trunk."

"What do you need it for?" I ask as the band members walk on the stage.

"I'm catching a cab home."

"I can't let you do that. That ride will probably cost $50."

"Money ain't a thing. Give me the keys."

"Okay, give me $50 and I'll drive you home."

"Daren, I'm not playing with you!"

"Baby, just chill for an hour and I'll drive you home after the show."

"GIVE ME THE FUCKIN' KEYS!"

With that outburst I stand and head for the door. Everyone in our section is still focused on us. I can't believe this shit. My watch reads 6:40 and as soon as we turn to walk out the gate, Erykah's voice sounds through the speakers. The crowd erupts with cheer and I want to be one of them. I would like to look into Erykah's pretty eyes and drift away. I try to peek back, but only catch a glimpse of Ms. Badu. "Bye, Erykah," I say as I proceed to the exit. If her purse wasn't in my car and my money wasn't in her house, I'd let her ass leave.

We stop right outside of the pier on a small brick wall. I lift Libra up so that she can have a seat and I begin calming her down. I take off her sandals and begin massaging her feet. She loves the envious looks coming her way and, as we talk, her smile returns. It is as beautiful as ever, but her feet don't look as good. We can still hear Erykah performing, but I disregard it being live until I see Common walk by us with Erykah's son. Yup, Erykah is here. I should accept Libra's offer to buy me a pair of tickets for her DC show.

Everything is cool now and we're holding hands walking back to my car. So my cutie-pie is a little insecure? Okay, she's very insecure. I hope she doesn't expect me to check in every five minutes when I'm not with her. I ain't about to be a sucka for her or anybody else. Shoot, without trust I can't make her my wife. Arriving at my car, I open the door for her, we get in and hit 95 South. Our ride is quiet and the radio is playing Aaliyah's "Rock The Boat." She is so smooth – I would like to see her in concert. This song now reminds me of being in the hotel with Shar-Baby.

"Daren, I can't believe you're so inconsiderate."

"What did I do now?"

"Who is this bitch you're seeing."

You're that bitch. Now shut the fuck up! I say to myself and I turn the volume up a little.

"Don't do that when I'm talking!"

I put "Big Pimpin'" back in and turn the volume all the way up. It plays on full blast until she closes her mouth. When she does I turn it down. She then tries to talk again so I turn it back up. Once she closes her mouth I turn it back down and she never talks again until we get to her condo. She got the message.

I immediately go to the canister above the refrigerator and retrieve the $300 I put in it.

"What are you doing?" Libra asks with a hint of confusion on her face.

"I'm leaving."

"You can't leave. I wanna talk."

She must be crazy if she thinks I want to hear anything that she has to say. "Libra, look, sweetie..." How do I say this? "Baby, it's been a long night and a lot of things were said that shouldn't have been, and there remains a lot of tension in the air. I think it would be best if we slept at different places tonight, calm down, get our minds right, and then we can talk tomorrow like adults." I now walk to the door.

"I wanna talk tonight," she says as she stands in front of the door and blocks my path.

"Baby, we talked at the concert and for about an hour outside of the concert."

"Well, there's more to talk about."

"We'll talk tomorrow," I say trying to open the door around her.

"No, you can't leave."

I pull the door softly, hoping that she'll move, but she won't budge. "Daren, I'm not going to make you stay if you want to leave."

"I can't tell...it looks like you're blocking me from leaving."

Libra pauses in thought and now steps aside. I open the door and walk down the first flight of stairs. I notice Libra looking down on me over the banister. "Daren, please stay."

"See you tomorrow."

"Fine!" she says with an attitude. "You wanna leave? Well take this with you!" and she quickly walks back into her condo.

"This is some real movie shit," I say aloud. "I can't believe this." Let me walk back up here and see what she's doing. I walk through the door to find all of my belongings, which include both things that she bought me and things that I bought her, sitting on the nook.

"Take all of your shit with you, Daren," she says appearing from her room with an armful of underwear and socks.

"Libra, why are you giving back things I bought you and things you bought me? Keep the gifts that I bought you."

"No! I don't want anything that reminds me of you. Just take it all and get out."

"Can I have a bag, please?" I ask sarcastically.

"I don't give a damn about no damn bag! Get one."

I go to the kitchen closet and get a big trash bag and put everything inside. I then walk to the front door and Libra immediately jumps up from the sofa and grabs my right arm.

"Please, don't leave me, Daren!" she says with pleading eyes and a miserable voice.

"You must have bumped your head when you were drunk the other night. Look, you showed your ass at the concert, you tried to raise your voice at me in my car, you done packed all of my shit and told me to get the fuck out, now you tell me to stay?"

"I'm sorry, Daren."

"This shit done got way out of hand. Just let go of my arm so I can leave."

"Daren, please listen –"

"Get the fuck off of my arm!" I yell and

I yank it from her grasp and walk out of the door. I'm now walking down the stairs and she's following me. As I reach the second floor she stands on the last step and grabs my arm again. I give her a stern look and she takes off up the stairs like a rocket. She might have a gun. Let me get the hell out of here.

CHAPTER 31

Daren drove to TGI Fridays. Normally he'd have an ice-cold draft beer, but that's for pleasure. Right now he needed a mudslide, which is a nice, frozen chocolate and vodka drink just to relax his mind and console his thoughts. He needed someone to talk to, but all of the women he's been seeing lately couldn't do much for his present situation. He decided to call Robin.

"Hello?"

"Robin, can you talk?"

"What's wrong, honey? You don't sound right."

"Come on out to the Fridays in Laurel so we can talk. I'm at the bar and your drinks and food are on me."

"It's that serious?"

"Yes, it is."

"Something concerning that woman you're seeing?"

"Yes."

"Dag! Y'all just got started. Okay, don't go anywhere. I'll be right there." Robin clicked the phone until she could hear a dial tone. She then dialed another number.

"Hello?"

"Girl, what are you doing?"

"Visiting my mother. I'll be there shortly."

"Don't come here. Look, Tammy, do you want your man back?"

"Robin, it's over between us."

"Not Donald! Your man, your real man. You know who I'm talking about."

"Daren? What are you talking about?"

"This is your chance so don't blow it. Daren is at the Fridays in Laurel at the bar. He sounds hurt and he called me to come talk to him. Some woman has messed his head up. Get down there and get your man."

Daren sat at the bar with an empty glass in front of him. The bartender took it and asked if he'd be having another. "No, thanks," Daren answered, "I'm waiting on a friend." He then took his eyes away from the bartender and put them back on the TV where ESPN was airing a baseball game. Suddenly he heard a soft voice over his shoulder.

"Is anyone sitting here?"

"Yes," Daren answered without looking at the woman.

"Well, I'll just sit here until she gets back.

Daren didn't feel like being bothered so he paid her no attention. He'd simply ask her to leave once Robin arrived.

"Do you care to talk about what's on your mind?" The woman asks. Daren acted as if she wasn't talking to him. "Daren."

He suddenly recognized the voice and turned to his right to find Butter sitting next to him. He gave a faint smile. "What in the world are you doing here? Where's Robin?"

"I came here in her place."

"Is that right?"

"Yes, but there's more. I came to give myself to you."

Daren looked at Butter like she was crazy. "Aren't you married? I know things ain't going right in your world, but I don't mess with married women. You know that."

"Daren, my marriage is over and there's no love there. It was a big mistake and it never would have happened if I had listened to my heart years ago. My heart was with you then, and it's still with you now. It will always be with you."

"Is that right?"

"Yes, it is. Is all you're going to say is 'Is that right?'"

"I'm sayin' though, you're married. Why are you here anyway?"

"I just told you that I'm here to give myself to you. I came to get what's mine."

"And that is?"

"You, my love, and my destiny."

Daren begins to laugh as Butter looks at him as if he's not. "Tamela –"

"Butter."

"Tamela –"

"Call me 'Butter', Daren."

"Anyway, you have a husband, a son and a stepdaughter, a mortgage or lease, car notes, and wedding rings and all that stuff. Don't bring all of that to the table talking about you're giving yourself to me. I don't want all of those things."

Butter paused, but didn't blink or back down. She was determined and she kept her focus. "I've filed for a divorce, the lease expires in two months, my stepdaughter is with her mother, I'm not wearing a wedding ring, and we do have a car note together, but that's no big deal. Plus, I'm living with Robin now."

"For real?"

"Yes. Daren, we are meant for each other and you know it. I've realized it and have stopped fighting it. Why don't you? I admit the truth and I'm finally listening to my heart."

"You admit that now and listen to your heart, but it's a little too late."

"Daren, I admitted it before, way back when we were kickin' it. I let you ease away then, but I won't now."

"Well, I gotta go. Tell Robin I said hi." Daren got up from the stool and began walking out of the restaurant. Butter followed.

"Daren, you can't hide from the truth and you can't run from what's real. Last time

I tried to get someone to take your place, but no one can replace you. I will not love another man or have sex with another man for the rest of my life. Only you will make my life complete. No other man will do!"

"The small group of people outside of the restaurant made it their business to focus their attention on Butter and Daren.

"Daren, please search your heart for your feelings. Don't continue living a lie and being mistreated by these other women. They don't know you like I do. They don't understand you like me. Daren, you always said that we only live once, so why would you want to live it without a woman that truly cares? Remember how I looked at you on my wedding day? You know me better than anyone. You could tell I was hurting. You knew I didn't want to marry him. You should have stopped me, but you didn't."

Daren was growing irritated of her calling his name and making a scene. First the scene at the concert, a couple of hours ago, and now the scene at Fridays – he couldn't take it any longer.

"Tamela, stop calling my name and go home."

"What about us? What about the DL Hughley concert we went to? What about going to see "Rush Hour" and all of those movies? What about the parks and the long strolls? What about us cuddled up watching TV all night?"

Daren had reached his tolerance limit. "What about the scene you made at the club? What about how ugly you acted when you slammed the door on my foot? Huh? What about how funky you acted at that picnic? Huh? You forgot about all of that? What about getting married to that clown and not waiting on me?"

Butter shot back, "What about Ocean City? What about my mother and my son? You know they're crazy about you. What about making love in the rain? What about making love over your cousin's house? What about the day we 'remet'? Remember I used to sit behind you in Mr. Lane's math class back in high school and I would call you BBD – Big Butt Daren because your butt was so perfect and juicy?"

"What do you want from me?!" Daren yelled in confusion.

"I want your love!" Butter yelled right back. "I want your love and your heart...I want my man." She then broke down crying like she never cried before right outside the doors of the restaurant.

Daren ran the short distance between them and grabbed Butter into his arms. "I apologize, Butter. Everything's going to be alright. My love is yours from this day forth." Daren felt his eyes get watery.

"Daren, all I want is your love...I just want you," Butter cried as she was embraced on the walkway to Fridays. "Am I asking too much?"

"No, baby. You're not asking too much. It's you and I from this point on. Your son is *our* son. Your world is *our* world. Shhh....calm down, baby. It's okay. It's going to be okay." Daren then began stoking her hair. "Sweetie, I wanted to stop you from getting married and I felt like a fool for not doing it. So much pain has happened in our lives because of me not stopping you that day. But it's time for the pain to stop and for the joy to begin. Butter...I love you."

"I love you, too," Butter replied as she looked up into Daren's eyes. It was the first time they had ever said those words to each other face to face, and the sound of them made Butter's knees buckle. Luckily for her, Daren held her firmly. As the two old lovers looked into each other's teary eyes, their faces met and a passionate kiss ensued. Everyone in front of the restaurant and in the window who witnessed the drama began to clap and cheer on the long kiss. Butter and Daren stood there and held each other for minutes and softly cried while feeling the realization that they were finally reunited.

CHAPTER 32

Two hours later Butter and Daren were in a suite at the Marriott. Daren lay across the bed with his body saturated with moisture while Butter sat straddled across him.

"You like that, baby?" she asked.

"Yes, baby. Work it. I've missed you so much." Daren winced with pleasure. "Butter, you do it so good."

"I'm just glad to be touching you again. Oops! I spilled some of your massage oil. This stuff smells good. Where did you get it from again?"

"This sistah that started her own lotions, oils, and candles business. She's very creative. This one is called *New Love*. That's ironic, ain't it?

"It sure is. Get me some next time you see her."

"Okay, baby."

"Now turn over so I can massage your chest. How does your back feel? Is it fine?"

"You did a good job, Butter."

After the massage, they both finished eating the food that they brought with them and watched a movie. Afterwards, they talked until the break of dawn. They lay there peacefully cuddled together, fully dressed. They experienced an exciting night of companionship, comfort, and conversation. They planned on attending the same church from that day forward, turning their lives over to Christ, and to be open and honest to one another every day of their lives. Making love to each other in the physical sense never crossed their minds.

CHAPTER 33

"Daren, where are you?"

"You know where I am?"

"You just had to go over there, didn't you?"

"You know it. Got a score to settle."

"Well, good luck. Will I see you when you're done?"

"I'll call later, Sexy," Daren said approaching the door. "I'm here now so let me talk to you later, baby."

"Bye, Handsome."

Daren knocks on the door, and as it swings open he walks in with strategic destruction on his mind and on his expression.

"You've been scared to come over here for a long time, ain't you? We ain't seen you since 1983. You ready for another ass whippin from the champs?"

Daren looked to Tasha on his right and knew what he had to do. He then looked at her partner Shannon on his left. Straight ahead was Deniese who was just returning to her seat at the table.

"Deniese, are you ready to handle this business and shut them up for another five or six years."

"You know I am, boo. You ready?"

"I'm ready, sweetie. Deal them cards. And Tasha and Shannon, I don't want y'all to be trying to give any hints or clues with your eyes; no winking, tapping, hitting feet under the table, or saying things like, 'Boy, you a *big jokester*,' or 'I got a *little joke* to tell.' Don't even try to cheat. We gonna be on y'all asses tonight."

An hour and a half later Deniese and Daren had 540 points while Tasha and Shannon only had 190.

"Things are back to normal up in here," Deniese laughed. We got in that ass, didn't we, Daren?"

"Hell yeah! They caught me at a bad time last game, but I'm back."

"Yeah, I was worried about you, boo. I'm glad to have my partner back."

Tasha was mad as hell. "What y'all doing next Friday?" she asks.

"Why?" Daren asks. "You wanna play some *Uno?* I know you don't want anymore Spades up in here."

"You get on my nerves, Daren, with your black ass. We would have won if Shannon ain't renege so many times."

"Oh, don't even try it!" Shannon yelled back. "You had the bomb hand twice and you ain't know how to play your cards. You kept cutting me!"

"Whateva!" Tasha rolled her eyes. "Whateva!"

CHAPTER 34

Butter stood at the door of the newly built, single family home and curiously watched two men play basketball on the court in the backyard. She couldn't believe how well they got along; it was almost as if they were good friends. She couldn't believe that they hadn't seen each other since high school, and they weren't even friends back then. She wondered what they were talking about. Butter never would have believed she'd see the day when her son's father William and her new man Daren would be getting along together in peace.

"Man, shoot the ball. Don't try to act like you Allen Iverson or Kobe or somebody out here just because your girl is watching. Don't forget who had that before you."

Daren smiled and shot the ball. "How can I forget that you had her first? I'm reminded of that fact every time I see your curly head son."

"That's right," Willie chuckled.

"I may have hit the pussy after you, but I hit it before your son."

"What you mean?" William asked in confusion. "You hit it while she was pregnant with my son?"

"No. You were with her then. I hit it a year before you got her pregnant. I mean way back when I was still in high school with y'all. Y'all had broken up for a few weeks."

"Bullshit!"

"I'm serious," Daren said as he tried to remain nonchalant about the facts. "If I would have put my mack down you wouldn't have had her after that point, and you never would have had a son by her."

"Whatever, nicca! Stop lying!" William grabbed the ball and stopped the game.

"Ask her."

William looked at Daren to see if he was joking, but Daren's expression didn't budge. William then motioned for Butter to open the screen door. "What do you call her?"

"Butter. That's some special shit between me and her. Only I can call her that. You wouldn't know nothin' 'bout that, playa."

William frowned. "Butter, did you and Daren fuck around back in high school?"

Butter opened the screen door. "What did you say?"

"Did you and Daren mess around back in high school?"

Butter rolled her eyes, smiled, and

closed the door. She was embarassed.

"You sneaky motherfucka! That's alright. I'm going to make my son knock on y'all's bedroom door whenever y'all close it. Y'all ain't never going to have no privacy." He and Daren began to laugh.

Butter was too through at William's question. She had heard enough silliness for one day. "Billy! Come here!" Billy came out of his room and stood in front of her. "Go outside and play basketball with your daddy and Loco." She knew that would stop their conversation. Maybe William's classless behind would continue talking about manly things, but Daren sure wouldn't talk about any of that stuff with Billy being so young.

"This is a nice house y'all bought," William commented. "Y'all got a basketball court, a nine-hole golf course, and a swimming pool. When I finish flippin' these keys I'm going to buy me a house."

"Don't pay for it in cash."

William smirked. "You think I'm stupid? I know how to do it." He then shot a three-pointer and it went in the hoop without touching the rim. "That's how you do it."

Billy then ran up on the court. "Can I play?"

"Yeah, you can play, son. You packed and ready to go?"

"Yes, Daddy."

"Go get your bag."

"Okay. Who's winning?" Billy asked.

"Loco's winning. Billy, we are going to teach your daddy how to play ball one of these days."

"Don't lie to my son. You're winning right now, but the game's just starting. If we had more time I'd beat you and you know it."

"Yeah, right," Daren said as he scored another basket.

"Loco, you still going to take me to a baseball game?"

"Billy, go get your bag so we can leave."

As Billy ran off, William held the ball. "Yeah, you taking him to a baseball game? You like baseball?"

"I'm not a big fan, but your son is. I told him I'd take him since he's always talking about it."

"Oh. Well, at least I know you'll take care of him and look out for him. That Donald motherfucka was seriously going to get killed. Was that shit you told me true? Was he really –"

"Gay? Hell yeah. He liked gettin' it in the ass more than he liked sexin' women. If that's his thing then it's his business, but don't be frontin' and actin' like you ain't and affecting other people's lives. This motherfucka got married knowing that he liked gettin' stuck."

When Billy returned, William and Daren shook hands and departed. William walked away a happy man. He knew he could trust that Daren would take care of Billy and not mistreat him, and he now had visitation whenever he wished. He also was paid up on his child support.

Daren walked the opposite direction just as happy. He now had his own home, a new car, and the right woman.

"Butter, get your pretty, gorgeous, beautiful, sweet ass out here."

"What, my handsome, chocolate lover?"

Daren took a knee next to the flowerbed and looked up to her. "Butter, the biggest mistake I've ever made was making you get off of your knee a few years back. Like you said, here's my chance to right some of the wrongs of my past. Butter, without you in my life I'll never be happy and satisfied...I'll never be whole. I need you in my life forever. Butter, will you –"

"Yes!" Butter screamed as she became weak in the knees. She began to cry and she kneeled down to hug Daren.

"Hold on, baby. Hold on. I wasn't finished. Will you marry me once your divorce is final?"

"Yes!" she screamed again. "Yes! Yes! Yes!" She pecked him on his lips with several quick kisses. "I'm yours."

"That's all I need to know. This is a promise ring for you. It's a diamond, but a promise ring – not an engagement ring."

"I understand," she said as she held her finger out for Daren to place it on her. "It's so beautiful. I love it!"

"That's good."

"So does this mean you're going to propose again when my divorce papers come?"
she blushed.

"Baby, that wasn't a proposal. You'll
know when I propose. You're going to have
to multiply what I just did to the tenth power."

Butter continued blushing. "I can't wait.
We haven't even made love yet."

"That's right. We're going to do it right
this time and wait till we get married."

"I'm going to tear you up on our honeymoon."

"I'll be looking forward to that night,
big balls and all."

"You are so silly. Damn, I'm lucky to
have you."

"Not lucky, but blessed."

"That's right, baby," Butter smiled. "I
love you."

"I love you, too. Come on, let's go celebrate."

"Where are we going? Baskin Robin's?
The Cheesecake Factory?"

"Let's go to Kings Dominion. No, Mi-
ami. No, Manhattan. Let's just go to LA or
Houston. Ooh, I also want to go to Memphis.
How about the Bahamas?"

"Wherever is fine with me, Daren. Let's
go."

"Go get our passports."

Once they got in the car, Daren put it in
first gear and took off down the street. "I

can't believe you got married to that fool anyway. Married to a straight up clown at that."

"I heard enough from Billy's father. Are you going to start up on me, too?" she began to smile.

"I mean, dag! How could he turn his back on a fine woman like you? If I slept with you every night and was married to you, I'd make sweet love to you constantly."

"I can't wait to be your wife."

"You know you're taking a blood test before I marry you, right? You've been with a man that ran up in other men with no condom and had men running up in him with no condom."

"I know you ain't talking! What about that crazy woman at the Erykah Badu concert? The one that you ain't wear a rubber with?"

Daren smiled and Butter snuggled up under him. "Anyway, my last name sounds much better on you than the one you have now."

"I agree. Change gears?"

"Yes, go 'head."

Butter reached down and changed the gears to Daren's stick-shift Corvette like he taught her to years ago. "I see that you have a couple of books up in here. What are you reading?"

"Nancey Flowers. I had to get a copy of her new book. Oh, Joylynn Jossel has a new novel out, too. I'll read one while you read the other."

"Sounds good to me. So where did a teacher get all of this money from?"

Daren glanced at her from the corners of his eyes and then looked back at the road ahead. "You have a choice – you can have $5,000 to go on a shopping spree while we're on this trip, or I can tell you where the money came from and you get nothing to shop with. And, before you answer, think of how many pairs of shoes and how many pocketbooks you can buy with the $5,000."

Butter paused in thought and couldn't help but to flash a huge smile. "Get ready to hold some bags because we're going shopping." They both laughed and smiled as Daren leaned down to kiss Butter on her lips. After the kiss she shifted the gears to fourth. "So where are we going?"

"All the way to the top if you ain't afraid," Daren responded as he stroked her hair and motioned for her to downshift. As they came to a stop at the red light, he ran down his CD options. "Okay, we got Gangstarr, Biggie, Jay-Z, Rick James, Dr. Dre, Mary J. Blige, India.Arie, Phyllis Hyman, Donny Hathaway, The S.O.S Band, LTD, Anita Baker, a Rare Essence tape back when they had Benny rappin', a new Backyard that's crankin', and Stevie Wonder. Oh yeah, I got some Yolanda Adams and Kirk Franklin. Eventually we'll cut back on all of this secular music."

"It don't seem like it."

"It takes time, sweetie. I'm only going to just listen to gospel and jazz one day."

"No Marvin Gaye?" Butter asked.

"Baby, I'm always going to listen to Marvin. He is always going to be up in here. As a matter of fact, I got three of his CDs in here now. But you know what? We can just cruise and talk."

"Let's do that. I love you, Daren."

"I love you, too, Butter."

The light turned green, Daren pressed the clutch, and as Butter shifted to first gear, Daren hit the gas and they never looked back.

Marlon Green's next novel Coming in 2004!

The atmosphere at the engagement party is one of warm spirits and love. Upon entering, Kerra and Jermaine made their rounds together and thanked every attendee. They were showered with hugs and smiles for everyone knew that this couple was a match made in heaven. After speaking with everyone, Jermaine went to sit with the men while Kerra went with the women.

"Kerra," says her friend Donna, "how did you and Jermaine meet? He is fine."

"Yeah, tell us how you two met," all of the other ladies chimed in.

"Okay, when I was down in Houston I got a job offer to work here so I took it. Every single day of my first week there, I would have a dozen of fresh, long-stemmed roses waiting on my desk; Monday's were yellow, Tuesday's white, Wednesday's peach, Thursday's pink, and Friday's red. I didn't know whom they were from. Well, some friends and I were out for lunch the following Monday when this tall, fine, handsomely built, chocolate man came to our table accompanied by two Mexican men. They both gave my friends a dozen of red roses, but Jermaine, who happened to be that tall, chocolate man, handed me three dozen, long-stemmed purple roses – a dozen for Saturday, Sunday, and Monday."

"Girl, look at you. After all of this time you're still blushing," says Allegera.

"Hold on," says Carmen, "you all haven't heard the best part yet. Tell them what Jermaine said to you. I was there, everybody," Carmen bragged. "I remember."

"Okay. I asked Jermaine who he was and why was he doing all of this and he said –"

"I'm all the man you need," Jermaine said butting into the conversation and reciting his words the exact way he originally delivered them a year ago. "I'm custom made for you, and your name is signed across my heart so it's exclusively yours. I honestly want you the right way and I'll do whatever it takes, within the good graces of your heart, to make you understand that we are meant to be. God has deemed that you are to be mine, and I will love you with every breath I take."

The hearts of all of the women sunk.

"Did he say it just like he did just now?" asked Allegera.

"Word for word," Kerra said dabbing the tears in her eyes to avoid her eyeliner from streaking. She stood and gave Jermaine a big hug and a kiss. "I told him that I had enough roses, but I would settle for some good conversation over dinner that night, my treat. We've been together ever since." She then gave him a more passionate kiss as she looked up into his eyes.

The women fanned themselves and filled the air with "Ooohs" and "Aaahs." They continued to shower them with positive comments and Kerra sat back down and ate up every bit of it while blushing. Jermaine rejoined the men.

"Why you gotta do romantic stuff in front of the other women?" Calvin said in a fed up tone. "Our women are now expecting us to come out the mouth with some corny shit."

"What?" Jermaine asked with an innocent look.

"Don't what us," Mike shot back. "You know what Calvin's talking about. You're always sweeping the ladies off their feet. How do you be doing that shit anyway?"

"How do I be doing what?"

"You know what I mean," Mike says. "Share your secrets with us. What's that thing you used to use on the girls?"

"*The Riley Technique*," Calvin blurts out. "I've been trying to get him to tell me how to do it since high school, but he won't tell nobody."

"Don't trip on your boys, Jermaine," says Mike. "You used to fuck all of the finest women. Come on and explain *The Riley Technique* to us. Don't front."

Jermaine smiled with a devilish grin. "We are too old for that nonsense."

Mike raised his brows. "Too old? You were just using it last year."

All of the men laughed in unison as Jermaine slapped hands with Mike in agreement with his statement.

"Come on guys," a woman called out, "we're about to bless the food."

"You're going to tell us when we get back over here," Mike said as the men joined the women and held hands. Jermaine just looked at him and grinned with thoughts of his promiscuous past. He stood at the head of the table with Kerra to his left, still grinning from ear to ear when she nudged him.

"Baby, what are you smiling about?" Kerra asked with a grin of her own.

"Nothing, sweetie-pie," Jermaine lied. The truth was that Jermaine's mind was surveying over all of the women that he slept with, sexed, made love to, and fucked. He felt like the luckiest man on earth because after all of his experiences, which included hundreds of women and thousands of condoms, he ended up without any kids, no sexually transmitted diseases, and found himself engaged to the sharpest woman he had ever seen. Being committed and monogamous had been easier than he thought. He was set on leaving the past behind him and that included sharing stories with his boys and also telling them the philosophy of *The Riley Technique. I will never tell. They would flip if they knew some of the women I'd been with, many women that they know very well*.

"I'll bless the food," LaPorsha stepped forward. "Y'all ready? Bow your heads...Dear Lord Jesus, we thank you for bringing us here, dear Lord Jesus, we ask that you bless the food that we are about to receive, dear Lord Jesus, please make it nourish and strengthen our bodies, dear Lord Jesus, and please...bless those that..." LaPorsha paused to compose herself, "please, bless those that couldn't be here. I'm sorry, everybody," LaPorsha blurted out, "but Nicole died earlier this year. I've been trying to hold it in and keep her death a secret, but I can't hold it in any longer."

Everyone looked up from their prayers as LaPorsha burst into tears and collapsed into Mike's arms.

"Our friend Niclole?" Kerra asked with a deep look of concern. "How did she die?"

"She died of AIDS. She didn't even know she had it."

"Oh my God," Kerra said as she looked on in a daze and squeezed Jermaine's left hand. "We were all so close." She turned to Jermaine for comfort. The tears that formed in her eyes disabled her from seeing the beads of sweat that appeared on his fore-head, but LaPorsha noticed them. As all eyes fell on her, she only paid close atten-tion to the sweat on Jermaine's forehead and the look of fear upon his face.

Jermaine tried his best to stay calm on the outside, but inside he was about to have a mental breakdown. Minutes ago he was in high spirits about his many triumphs, but LaPorsha wiped out those thoughts. Out of the many women that he laid down with, he failed to use a condom only once and that one time was with the last woman he was with before he met Kerra. That last woman was Nicole Watkins.

The big day is approaching, but Jermaine Riley must confess. As Kerra takes matters into her own hands, it turns out that there is plenty of confession to go around. Nei-ther of them, nor you, can imagine the real drama that lies far beyond the eyes!

Coming in 2004!
The True Confessions of...

Greenday Publishing Presents...

A Suspense Thriller from

Adrian Salmon

A Streetside Story from

Chloe Barksdale

the first lady of Greenday Publishing

Poetic Endeavors from

Mind Evolution

The Art of Seduction

An Intimate Journey from

Marlon Green and Friends

and

*The True Confessions of...*from

Marlon Green

You Won't Believe What's To Come!